DENVER MUSIC

E.D.G. SMITH

CHAPTER 1

Tuesday, 7 June 1881: "I hope you can get us a good room in Denver, Ma," said Audrey, turning away from the stagecoach. "Brad and I will take care of the bags."

"I'll take good care of Brad and Audrey, Mrs. Benton," promised Deputy Sheriff Dan Black. Abigail Benton, Abby to most everyone, left the stage office and headed toward the hotel.

"I'll stack our bags by the wall," said Brad, but he stopped, a bag in hand, looking intently at the door of the bank next to the stage office.

Two men ran out of the bank, guns drawn, and mounted their horses, which were standing close to the stagecoach. Two more men with drawn guns followed them out of the bank.

"Get down, Audrey! They're robbing the bank," warned Brad, pulling his sister down onto the boardwalk with him.

"It's a lawman! Get him," shouted one of the robbers through his mask, as he pointed his pistol at Deputy Black.

"I'll get him!" yelled another robber, taking a couple of shots at the deputy sheriff.

Dan Black started shooting at the robbers from the

boardwalk. A third robber was the first to get hit, as he mounted his horse. The man dropped his pistol, clutched at his saddle horn, and fell to the street.

As the deputy was taking aim at another one of the robbers, a bullet from one of the robber's pistol struck him. The deputy fell to his knees, but he held on to his pistol. Taking careful aim, the wounded deputy shot back.

"I'm hit," yelped another of the robbers, clutching his side. "But I'll make it. Let's go."

The three men spurred their horses to a gallop down the street, taking the fallen robber's riderless horse with them.

Brad watched them gallop away and rushed to Deputy Black, who was now flat on his back on the boardwalk. Pulling off his kerchief, Brad pressed it to the wound, stopping the bleeding.

"I'll help this one!" Audrey shouted to her brother, removing the wounded robber's kerchief and then pressing it against his wound. "What's your name?"

"Virgil."

"Virgil," said Audrey, "I have to remove your gunbelt. It's obstructing the wound." Audrey unbuckled the gunbelt and pulled it free. Picking up the pistol, she pushed it into its holster and placed it by her side, away from Virgil's reach. "Don't move; we'll get you to a doctor as soon as we can."

"Careful, lady! My partners are coming," he groaned as he reached for her. "I don't want you to get hurt."

Seven other men, guns drawn, rushed out of the bank and mounted their horses. Another robber looked through his mask at the two men lying in the street as Brad and Audrey bent over them.

"She's got Virgil's gun," shouted a robber, pointing his pistol toward Audrey. "I'll get her."

Audrey heard the shot and felt a bullet whiz past her. "Don't shoot!" she shouted. "I'm helping your partner. He's hurt pretty bad." Virgil didn't wait for another shot; he limply raised his arm, waved to his partners, and pulled Audrey down beside him.

"I'll get the hero helping the deputy," said one of them trying to aim his pistol and control his frightened mount at the same time.

Brad heard the first bullet whiz past, so he quickly fell to the ground. As he fell, a second slug ripped through his shirt, gouged his side, and buried itself in the street.

A ripple of gunfire erupted from the bank as one the bank's customers, rancher Brett Grimes, began shooting at the escaping robbers.

A robber teetered back on his skittering mount, dropping his pistol as he fell to the dusty street. Another of the rancher's bullets found its mark, and one more robber clutched his side. The wounded man gripped his horse's reins as he held his side, staring at Audrey. Another robber, his trousers wet with blood from a bullet in the thigh, grabbed the reins of his partner's riderless horse.

The gang's leader, heard the rancher's gunfire, drew his six-shooter, and fired back. During the exchange of gunfire, one of the rancher's bullets hit the kerchief masking the leader's face, knocking it down. His six-shooter empty, the rancher wisely ducked back into the bank for cover.

Audrey raised her head as the gunfire closed and her eyes met the gang leader's. His cold, emotionless eyes stared at Audrey as he pulled his kerchief back up. She shivered as their eyes briefly met.

"Come on, let's get out of here!" shouted a robber, spurring his horse down the street. "Virgil and Jesse are gone." The remaining robbers galloped after him, leaving Brad and Audrey bent over two wounded men. The third man lay sprawled in the street, bleeding.

"I'd like three beds," said Abby. "That can be one room or two rooms; I have my son and daughter with me."

"I'm short of rooms," replied the clerk, "but I can give you one large room, with two beds. It's a corner room, in the shape of an L. That's the best I can do."

"I understand, said Abby, "that will do. I'm here for ten days; I'm studying with Percival Vaughan-Williams, the organist at the Episcopal Church."

"Yes, a superb musician. You may be playing at his recital on the 16th of June. My name is George Girard, I sing in his choir."

"Why, that sounds like gun shots!" exclaimed Abby, turning her head toward the door.

There were a couple of thuds, and a piece of woodwork splintered above the clerk's head. "On the floor!" he shouted. "Everyone get on the floor!"

"They're robbing the bank!" yelled a man running through the door. He looked around the lobby, and then quickly hid behind a large chair.

8

"Who's robbing the bank, Nyle? Which bank?" shouted George Girard from behind the counter.

"The bank by the stage office," yelled Nyle. "And there's a young blond lady and a dark-haired young man treating the wounded."

"My children!" screamed Abby, getting to her feet as another bullet thudded into the hotel door. "Those are my children treating the wounded!"

A large man quickly stood up, grabbed Abby, and pulled her back down to the floor, covering her with his body. Several more bullets thudded into the hotel lobby, as gunfire and screams of horses broke the afternoon's tranquility.

"You can't help your children if you get yourself shot, ma'am. Wait until the shooting is over. I'm sure your children are doing everything you and your husband taught them to do in a dangerous situation."

"I'm sure they are, Mr....?" said Abby, waiting for the man to tell her his name.

"William, William Crawford," he replied. "And your name, ma'am?"

"Abigail Benton. And my children do know what to do in a dangerous situation, but they've never been in the middle of a gun battle, although their father has."

"Civil War, I presume, Mrs. Benton."

"You presume correctly."

"And you?"

"Civil War, Union Army," he replied.

They heard more gunfire, then the clatter of approaching horses as the robbers galloped down the street. When the sound faded away the hotel guests slowly got to their feet.

"Thank you, Mr. Crawford," said Abby, standing up, "but now I must check on my children."

Abby picked up the hem of her dress, rushed out the door and ran down the boardwalk to the stage depot. She saw men coming out of the bank, the stage depot, and surrounding businesses. In the middle of the street she saw Audrey, her blond hair glistening in the sunlight, bent over a man sprawled in the street. Not far away, she saw Brad, his hand pressed against the side of a man lying on the boardwalk. But worse, she saw blood on the side of her son's shirt.

CHAPTER 2

"Brad!" she screamed, rushing toward him. "You've been shot!"

"I'm okay, Ma, it's just a crease. But we need to get Deputy Black to a doctor right away. I've stopped most of the bleeding, but he needs a doctor now. Without a doctor he'll die."

"We can use my buckboard," offered a man in dirty overalls. "The hospital isn't far from here."

Sheriff Strong ran up to the knot of men standing around Brad and Audrey. "Someone going to tell me what happened?"

"A gang of outlaws just robbed the bank," answered rancher Brett Grimes. "We hit three or four of them; two are in the street."

"Let me help," volunteered a tall, dark-haired woman lifting up her long dress as she ran up to the sheriff. "I'm a Christine McLean, a nurse."

"Deputy Black needs a doctor now," Brad advised her. "I've stopped most of the bleeding, but he was hit in the side. I know he's bleeding internally."

Quickly taking charge, the nurse pointed at two men and said, "Pick him up and lay him in the buckboard. Be very gentle so the wound isn't aggravated. The rate of bleeding must not be increased."

"This is Virgil Collins," said Audrey. "The bullet went all the way through his side; I've stopped the bleeding."

Nurse McLean pointed at two other men who then picked him up and laid him beside Deputy Black.

Sheriff Strong stood over the other wounded bank robber and looked him in the eyes. "Well, Jesse, I told you it would end this way. You're lying in a street, shot full of holes, and your arm looks pretty bad."

"We'd have made a clean getaway if that crazy rancher hadn't started shooting," he groaned.

"If your ears had been open when I, your Ma, and your priest told you what to do and what not to do, you could have had a good life. Now you're facing prison, if you live. And if you do live, your arm is never going to work right again."

"Let me stop that bleeding," ordered Nurse McLean, pressing her handkerchief against a bullet hole in Jesse's leg. "I need some cloth strips or kerchiefs. Now!" she shouted.

Several men whipped off their kerchiefs and handed them to her. She quickly wrapped one around the wounded arm and tied it firmly. "This arm will never work right again; the bone is shattered. Your leg was more fortunate, it looks like a clean hole, so you should be able to walk. I don't know about the damage inside your body. Only the doctor can tell once he removes the bullets." She stood and nodded to the men who had watched her bandage Jesse Rebhorn.

"We'll add him to the buckboard, ma'am," responded a young cowboy, grasping Jesse's legs as Deputy Sheriff Jim McMurray grasped the wounded outlaw under the arms.

12

A cowboy climbed onto the wagon seat just before the farmer released the brake and slapped the reins. The team started at a slow walk, increasing speed when the farmer slapped the reins again. Everyone watched until the wagon was out of sight, and then the crowd slowly dispersed.

"Well, the bad guys were pretty bold today," concluded Sheriff Strong, as he picked up Virgil's gunbelt and Jesse's six-shooter. "Jim, get a posse together and follow them. We've got two of their men so we'll soon know about the rest of them. Be careful; don't let anyone get shot. We've already got three wounded and one of them is my deputy."

"I've already got some volunteers, Sheriff," said Deputy McMurray. "We're meeting in front of your office; should be on our way in a few minutes."

"Let me check your side, young man," the nurse interjected firmly.

"It's just a crease, ma'am, but it really stings," said Brad.

Nurse McLean examined Brad's side, nodded in agreement, and said, "Stop by the hospital later this afternoon and let one of the doctors check it. Consider that an order, understand? You can check on your friend, Deputy Black, at the same time."

"Yes, ma'am."

"Before you go, I need you to tell me about the robbers," said the sheriff. "The two of you were closest to the gang. Did either of you get a good look at any of them?"

"I did," said Audrey, her voice soft but firm. "The leader's mask fell from his face and he looked at me.

13

No, he didn't look at me, he stared through me. It was scary."

Nurse McLean interrupted, "Sheriff, the man that you were talking to appears to be in pretty bad shape. He's the one the rancher shot."

"That makes sense," said the sheriff. "Grimes is a good shot, and he isn't hesitant to use his gun when in a dangerous situation. But back to the robbers; miss, can you come by my office?"

"My name is Audrey Benton. This is my brother, Brad, and my Ma," Audrey replied. "And yes, we'll come to your office."

"Thank you, Miss Benton. Say about six o'clock? I need you to look at some wanted posters."

"We'll be there," Mrs. Benton agreed. "That will give us time to go to the hotel and then the hospital."

"Fine. I'll see you at six."

Brad and Audrey picked up their bags and followed their mother down the boardwalk and into the hotel. Abby signed the register, and Mr. Girard gave her the room key.

The Bentons entered their hotel room and placed their bags on the floor. "It may be just a scratch, young man, but I'm going to clean and bandage that scratch," said his mother.

"Yes, Ma." Brad carefully removed his shirt.

"It is just a scratch," confirmed his sister.

"I'm still going to clean it," declared their mother. "Audrey, bring that pitcher of water and basin over here to the night stand."

Abby cleaned the wound with soap and water, despite

Brad insisting that the doctor would be examining the wound in less than an hour.

"He can examine and doctor the wound," said Mrs. Benton. "But as your mother, I'm going to clean and bandage it. I'd rather have that scratch over-doctored than under-doctored."

"Yes, Ma," sighed Brad, resigned to his mother's attentions.

They unpacked, changed into fresh clothes, and went downstairs. While Audrey and their mother took their time looking over the ornate lobby, Brad asked Mr. Girard directions to St. Joseph Hospital.

"There's the hospital," said Audrey.

"Right where Mr. Girard said it would be," confirmed Brad.

Brad opened the door, and the three of them entered. The waiting room had a clean, freshly scrubbed smell with the subtle odor of soap. Mrs. Benton stopped at the desk where a nun was writing.

"Excuse me," she said. "My son was shot earlier this afternoon, and Nurse Christine McLean told him to stop by and see a doctor.

"Yes, Mrs. Benton. Take the left hallway and go to room 104. The doctor will be with you shortly."

"How did you know my Ma's name?" asked Brad.

"Nurse McLean told me to expect you, and you fit her description of a young man with black hair with a blond sister and mother."

"Abby, Brad, Audrey," greeted Nurse McLean, entering the reception area. "Room 104 is one of our larger examining rooms. I'll tell the doctor you're here, and then I'll come get things ready for him."

They entered the examining room and looked around. "It's kind of like Doc Adams' office, except there are more bottles and instruments," observed Brad.

"Brad," said Nurse McLean as she entered the room, "Please remove your shirt, and lie down on the examining table. Dr. Ben Eckstein has just finished with Deputy Black. He wants to check your wound and update you on the deputy's condition."

Brad unbuttoned his shirt, wincing when he stretched his arm to take it off. He sat on the edge of the table, and then lay down.

"Nurse McLean," queried Brad, "Why are there nuns working in the hospital? I've heard about nuns and their black and white uniforms, but this is the first time I've ever seen one."

"Saint Joseph Hospital was founded by an order of nuns, the Sisters of Charity. Their uniforms are called habits; I don't know why, but I'm sure there's a reason."

"But why did they start a hospital?"

"The Sisters of Charity is an organization of Roman Catholic women who have dedicated their lives to the church doing charitable works. In this case they founded a hospital. They came here from Leavenworth, Kansas about 13 years ago."

"We'll have to ask Father O'Brien about them when we return to Riverton," said Audrey.

"Father Trevor O'Brien?" asked a passing nun from the doorway.

"Why, yes," responded Audrey.

"Is he perhaps from Chicago?" she asked.

16

"Yes, said Brad. "Do you know him?"

"Yes, I'm from Chicago; I know him and his sister. Please tell him Sister Teresa said hello." With that, the young nun glided away as silently as she had appeared.

"Are nuns always that quiet?" asked Brad.

"None are as quiet as Sister Teresa. She was trained in nursing by Sister Joanna Bruner, the first trained nurse in the Sisters of Charity. She was also the first trained nurse in the State of Kansas."

"How long has she been in Denver?" asked Brad.

"A little over five years; she arrived when the hospital was still on Market Street. Market Street is one of the, shall I say, less proper areas of Denver. But enough of that. Now, turn on your side so the doctor can examine your wound."

"Yes, ma'am."

"Now," she asked as she removed the bandage, "Who taught you two how to doctor?"

"How to doctor?" laughed Audrey. "We just stopped the bleeding to keep the men alive until they got to a doctor."

"Well," said a small, balding man standing in the doorway, "you saved the lives of two men. You did everything but remove the bullets. I call that pretty good doctoring. I'm Ben Eckstein, one of the hospital's doctors."

Abby Benton gripped the doctor's hand, "Thank you," she said. "Their father and I have shown them how to bandage and to stop wounds from bleeding."

"Brad, I'll check your wound while I tell you about Deputy Black and the two bank robbers," said Dr. Eckstein. Nurse McLean moved away from Brad so the

17

doctor could examine the wound. "Deputy Black will be up and around by the end of the week, thanks to you stopping the bleeding. If you hadn't stopped the bleeding when you did, that wouldn't be the case."

"Thank you," gasped Brad as the doctor dabbed the wound with a carbolic acid solution.

"That usually smarts a mite," confirmed the doctor.

"Pa didn't flinch when we daubed his wound with it," recalled Brad. "I don't know how he kept so quiet."

"You used a carbolic acid solution on your Pa? When was this?"

"When we found him after he'd been shot by Duke Badger and left to the wolves in a snowstorm," said Audrey suddenly flooded with emotion. She choked back a sob as she recalled finding their father.

"That was your Pa, and you are the two who rescued him?" exclaimed the doctor. "I'd heard about that, and now I've met the two children who saved their Pa! Tell me about it, from the beginning."

As Brad and Audrey told the story, Nurse McLean and Dr. Eckstein nodded and asked questions. Tears trickled down their mother's face as the story progressed. Mr. Benton turned to face the wall, using her handkerchief to dab the tears from her eyes.

There was a pause after they finished telling their tale. Audrey broke the silence, "I helped Sarah Davis, Doc Adams' new nurse, deliver a baby a few months ago."

"I see," said Dr. Eckstein. "Well, you're on your way to becoming a doctor. Not many women doctors yet; you'll be one of the first. Don't give up. It will be a tough challenge, but you have a gift for medicine. Virgil

Collins is alive because of you. Come back this evening and Deputy Black may be up to seeing visitors. I'll tell the receptionist to put you on his approved visitor's list; same for the robbers Virgil Collins and Jesse Rebhorn. I've got to make my rounds now. It was a pleasure to meet a young hero and heroine."

Dr. Eckstein quickly departed. Nurse McLean motioned them to follow her back to the reception area. "There is no charge for Dr. Eckstein's services," she said. "The city will pay because you were wounded while treating Deputy Black."

Brad walked a little slower than usual as they returned to the hotel. Audrey looked at him and remarked, "Brad, you look a little peeked. The wound hurts, doesn't it?"

"Yes, it still smarts a mite, especially when I walk fast."

"We've got plenty of time," said their mother. "There's no need to hurry."

"You could take a nap when we get back to the room," Audrey suggested. "We have some free time before we meet Sheriff Strong at six o'clock."

"I'd like that. I wonder how many wanted posters he has."

CHAPTER 3

Tuesday evening, 7 June, 1881: "Well, it's six o'clock and you're right on time," greeted Sheriff Strong. The sheriff was drinking coffee, sitting at his desk with two piles of posters in front of him. "I've been looking through the Wanteds, and this is a stack of the most likely men."

Brad took the stack of posters, placed it on the table under the gun rack, and started turning over the posters slowly, one by one. "Tell me if you recognize one," he said to his sister.

Several minutes later, Audrey placed her hand on her brother's arm, stopping his poster-turning. "That's one of them," she said, picking up one of the posters, "Jake Rawlins."

"Jake Rawlins," said the sheriff. "He used to run with the Badger Gang."

"We know about the Badger Gang," responded Brad, "Don't we Audrey?"

"Yes, we know them very well, unfortunately."

The sheriff looked up at them and asked, "Pray tell, how do you younguns know about the Badger Gang?"

Brad and Audrey told the sheriff about Duke Badger taking their father captive and how they had tracked the gang after the unsuccessful efforts of Sheriff

Tate and his posse. Audrey's voice broke when they described finding their father, armed only with a stick and surrounded by wolves getting ready to attack him.

"So, you shot the wolves as the blizzard was starting?" questioned the sheriff.

"That's right," said Brad. "Then we bandaged his wounds and built a shelter before the storm got really bad."

"Duke hadn't fed Pa for a couple of days," added Audrey. "Then he took Pa's boots and coat, shot him, and rode away. That's when we came to the top of the hill and saw Pa armed only with a stick."

"Well, thank goodness Duke Badger is gone," said the sheriff. "However, we still have men around that rode with him in the past, including Jake Rawlins. Rawlins has been seen in this area, but he hasn't been involved in any holdups or robberies. He's had solid alibis every time one has taken place. I had every reason to believe him when he said he was going straight."

"Jake Rawlins is definitely the man," asserted Audrey. "He looked right at me. No, he didn't look at me; he stared at me, or through me. I felt a cold chill when he did." She turned to Brad and continued, "It was the same feeling I had when you shot the wolf while I was getting water after we found Pa. The wolf stared right through me, just like Jake Rawlins did this afternoon."

"There have been a number of holdups over the past year," remarked the sheriff. "It's beginning to look like they may have been done by Rawlins and his gang. And now that you've identified him, I'm concerned about your safety, Miss Benton."

"About my safety?"

"Yes, your safety. You're the one eyewitness that can connect him with the robbery. You said he stared at you after his kerchief dropped. He may come after you. That's why I'm concerned."

"Thank you for the warning," said Brad. "We'll talk to Ma when we get back to the hotel and decide what we should do."

"I'll say nothing about Audrey recognizing Jake Rawlins,". "I'll also let the word out that the two wounded outlaws have refused to name other gang members. I don't think it will take long for that to get back to Rawlins."

"Well, Ma does have a .32 pistol in her purse," divulged Audrey. "And she's a good shot with it, too."

"I hope she doesn't have to use it," replied the sheriff. "Miss Benton, while you're in Denver, don't go anywhere alone. I want you to be with your brother or your mother at all times. Do you understand?"

"Yes, sir."

"I'll stick to her closer than a bear to a honey pot," vowed Brad.

"Now go back to the hotel and enjoy dinner with your Ma. The hotel restaurant is a right nice place to eat."

"We're ready for dinner, agreed Brad. "But first we're going to see Deputy Black. Ma is meeting us at the hospital at half-past six."

"Dr. Eckstein said he'd put us on the approved visitor list," explained Audrey.

"Well, you'd better hurry," chuckled Sheriff Strong. "The dining room usually fills up by half-past seven."

Brad and Audrey left the sheriff's office, heading to Franklin Street and Saint Joseph Hospital.

"You're on the list of approved visitors," said the receptionist looking up from a sheet of paper on her desk. Pointing to the hall on her left, she continued, "Dan Black is down that hall, Room 151."

"Thanks, ma'am," replied Brad.

The three Bentons quickly reached Room 151. Brad knocked gently on the already open door and said, "Deputy Black, it's Audrey and Brad Benton, and Ma is with us."

"Brad," said the wounded deputy, looking up. "Please come in. How are you feeling? Dr. Eckstein said you were wounded too."

"It was just a crease," explained Audrey, "but he does have to walk carefully. But more important, how are you?"

"The doc said I have Brad to thank for some excellent emergency medical care. So I say, thank you Brad, for saving my life."

Brad's face reddened, then said, "You're welcome, but I just did what you would have done."

"Well, I'm glad you did it. Christine McLean said you did the right things quickly. I don't think I would have done that well under the circumstances."

"Their Pa and I trained both of them," explained Mrs. Benton. "And that training has saved several lives so far, including their father's after he was shot by Duke Badger."

"I heard about that," said the deputy, looking carefully at Brad and Audrey. "Then you're the two youngsters that tracked the Badger Gang and saved their father. It's an honor to meet you, and to be the third life that you saved. Tell me about it."

Brad and Audrey recounted the story for the third time that day, including the part about Audrey breaking the jaw of the gang member they had captured. And, as happened every time the story was told, their mother had to daub her tears with a handkerchief.

After the story, Deputy Black broke the silence. "The two wounded outlaws survived. Jesse Rebhorn will live. The doc saved his right arm, but his shooting days are over. Hopefully, he'll have some use of his arm when he recovers."

"What about Virgil Collins?" asked Audrey.

"He asked about you," replied the deputy. "Why don't you go see him? He's a few doors down on the other side of the hall."

After Brad and Audrey told the deputy about their visit with Sheriff Strong and the Wanted posters, the Bentons said their good-byes and went in search of Virgil Collins.

"Mr. Collins?" said Audrey, looking at the outlaw on the bed. His good arm was handcuffed to a chain connected to the metal bed frame. "Deputy Black said you were asking about me."

"Yes, I was. Thank you for saving my life. You were doing a decent act by helping me. I'm sorry my partners shot at you."

"Even though you robbed the bank, I couldn't let you bleed to death. It was the right thing to do."

"Right thing?"

"Yes," said Audrey. "It was the Christian thing to do, ask the hospital chaplain about it when he visits you."

Mr. Collins studied Audrey for several moments, then he turned toward Brad. "Christians are supposed to help bank robbers?"

"Yes," said Brad. "Talk to the chaplain; he'll answer all your questions."

"I just might do that," he said, motioning towards his handcuffed arm. "The doctor said I'm going to be here about a week or so before I'm transferred to the jail. And again, thank you for saving my life. Maybe I'll be able to do the same for you some day."

The Bentons said their goodbyes, left the hospital, and began their walk back to the hotel. Brad and Audrey started talking through the events of the day.

"Ma, the shooting was over when I helped Deputy Black," explained Brad. "I didn't know there were still robbers in the bank."

"Mr. Collins pulled me down after the first shot was fired," added Audrey. "He protected me."

"You both did the right thing," sighed their mother, stopping and looking at them. "It's just," she paused, looking at the mountains still capped with snow. "You're my children. I don't want you hurt. I thought I'd never see your Pa again after Duke Badger took him. And now, my son has been shot, if only a crease. And, to make matters worse, my daughter's life may be in danger because she recognized the leader of the gang."

Audrey looked at her mother, "Sheriff Strong said he's going to spread the word that he has no leads. He's also going to tell people that no one was able to identify any of the robbers, and that the two wounded men refuse to talk."

"Well, I'm your mother, and mothers are supposed to worry about their children. And I'm going to be the dutiful worried mother until we're safely back in Riverton."

♘

Hotel Dining Room, 7:30 P.M.: The waiter arrived at the Bentons' dinner table with a large platter of food. He carefully placed a plate with trout and fresh vegetables in front of Mrs. Benton, then an identical plate in front of Audrey. He placed a plate with a large steak, vegetables, and boiled potatoes in front of Brad. "Will that be all, ma'am?" he asked, looking at Abby.

"Yes, and the food looks marvelous."

As soon as the waiter left, they gave thanks and began eating. Brad looked around at the ornate draperies, stopping to peer at the large chandelier in the center of the room. Audrey turned her head and looked too, then turned to her brother.

"That is a big chandelier," she commented.

Brad nodded in agreement as he continued to examine it. "Mr. Acker said it was a nice hotel, and to be sure and look at the drapes and chandeliers in the dining room; he was right when he said the chandeliers are really something to behold."

"The food is marvelous, too," added Audrey. "It's as good as the trout we caught when we were tracking Pa. What did they do to make it taste so good, Ma?"

Abby took a small piece of the fish and gently savored

it before answering. "I can taste butter, garlic, onion, and," she paused, "and, I believe, some type of cheese."

"Cheese?" questioned Brad.

"Yes," said his mother thoughtfully, "cheese. Maybe the waiter can tell us about it when he returns."

Audrey tasted her fish carefully, and then said, "Yes, I taste cheese, too. It's not cheddar, but it is cheese."

"Well," professed Brad, "this kind of Pinkertoning I could really be good at. What kind of cheese? It's sounds a lot safer than the tracking the Bigfoot Gang, Duke Badger, fighting fires, or capturing a fake healer."

"Let's not think about those bad events of the past," admonished their mother. "I'm here to study with Percival Vaughan-Williams and you're here to have a vacation. What with all your Pinkertoning and capturing outlaws, you deserve some time to learn things and see the big city of Denver."

"Denver is big," agreed Brad.

Audrey slowly put her hand on her brother's arm, pulling him toward her, and then whispered in his ear. "Brad, keep examining the chandeliers and drapes. But, in a minute I'd like you to find an excuse to look behind yourself. There's a man that keeps looking at me. He's tall, with light brown hair, and he has a large, round, head. And don't tell Ma; there's no reason to get her upset."

"What secrets are you telling your brother?" teased her ma.

Just then, Brad saw a young lady with long black hair leaving the dining room with a man and woman, probably her parents. "Audrey was telling me that the young lady with the long black hair had looked at me several times. But don't worry, Ma, I think she was just admiring the drapes. I'm too young for her."

"I'm glad you realize that," replied his mother. "I know some boys your age are getting married, but you need to wait until you finish high school, and hopefully college, before you think about marriage. Marriage is a big responsibility."

"Yes, Ma. That's why Audrey and I saved the money from the rewards, so we can go to college."

"That's right, Ma, we're planning on going to college."

"I see you dropped your napkin, Audrey, I'll get it," said Brad, discreetly pulling the napkin off his sister's lap. He pushed his chair back and knelt beside his sister to pick up the napkin. Now he could see the man with the large head. While kneeling, he continued, "What a beautiful fireplace! I wouldn't have seen it if you hadn't dropped your napkin."

"Good things can come from mistakes," responded their mother. "And that is an interesting fireplace; you're very perceptive, just like your father."

"Thank you, Ma," said Brad. "The light brown wood trim above the large round stones is unusual."

"I'm glad you could see it," said his sister. "I was going to point it out to you."

Dessert time finally arrived, and the waiter suggested the German chocolate cake, a specialty of the chef. Mrs. Benton declined, but did agree to take a bite of Audrey's cake. "But before you leave," said Mrs. Benton, "can you tell me what kind of cheese the chef put on the trout?"

"Yes, ma'am," said the waiter. "Many people have asked me that question. The chef sprinkles a little grated Parmigiano Reggiano cheese on the fish. His brother, also a chef, is at the Palmer House in Chicago. His brother sends him the cheese, which is imported."

"That sounds Italian," said Audrey.

"It is. We usually call it parmesan, though, rather than Parmigiano Reggiano, because parmesan is easier to say. The cheese is aged for two years, first at around 60 degrees, then at around 50 degrees. When the cheese arrives from Italy, it is in the shape of a drum and weighs about 50 pounds."

"Fifty pounds is a lot of cheese. How do you use it all?" asked Abby.

"We sell some of it to other fine restaurants in Denver, such as the Silver Platter," said the waiter.

"Thank you," said Abby. "I'll ask David Acker if he can get me some."

"Mr. Acker, of the Riverton Hotel?" questioned the waiter.

"Why, yes," said Abby. "Do you know him?"

"Only by reputation," said the waiter. "He's friends with the owner of this hotel. But please excuse me, I'll be right back with your dessert."

A few minutes later the waiter returned with one slice of cake for Audrey, and two slices for Brad. The waiter explained, "One of the slices is broken, so I'm not supposed to serve it. However, I told the chef that you were a friend of David Acker and that you wouldn't object to an extra slice, even if it was broken."

"No," agreed Brad, a large smile on his face, "I won't object."

They talked about the chandeliers, the drapes, and the ornate moldings in the dining room as they ate their dessert. When they finished, Abby paid for their dinner and they left the dining room.

"The lobby is beautiful," observed Audrey as she looked around. "It's very impressive."

"It is lovely," agreed their mother as they climbed the stairs to the second floor.

"The hallway is so long," said Brad. "The window at the end of the hall overlooks a balcony. The doorman told me that the end rooms have a door that opens directly onto the balcony. The guests in those rooms can take a chair onto the balcony and watch the city below."

"It is a lovely hotel," said their mother as they reached their door. "That's why Mr. Acker recommended we stay here."

Mrs. Benton unlocked the door. Brad entered first, lit the kerosene lamp, and then looked around the room. "What are you doing?" asked his mother.

"Just checking out the room," replied Brad. "Nana said I should check to make sure someone else hadn't accidentally mistaken our room for theirs."

"She did say that, didn't she?" confirmed his sister, nodding in agreement.

"I don't recall my mother saying that. But it is getting late, and we're the only ones in this room. Let's get to bed; I have to be at the church early tomorrow morning for Mr. Vaughan-Williams. This is your bed, by the door, Brad. Audrey and I will share the bed around the corner."

"Yes, Ma," said Brad as he closed and locked the windows. "I'll see you in the morning." When their mother had gone around the corner, Brad continued.

"Audrey, while Ma's getting ready for bed, will you help me take off my shirt? The wound still smarts."

"It probably hurts because you ate all that cake," she chided. Brad took the straight-back chair by his bed and braced it against the doorknob. Audrey nodded in approval and then helped him off with his shirt.

"Good night, Brad."

"Good night, Audrey," just before he blew out the kerosene lamp.

CHAPTER 4

Wednesday, 8 June 1881: The three Bentons were finishing their breakfast at the hotel cafe, talking, and looking out the window at the horses and wagons passing by.

"That man is watching me again," Audrey whispered. "He's walking out the door now."

"I see him," replied Brad.

"What are you two whispering about now?" asked their mother.

"Uh, about your music lesson," said Brad a little too quickly.

"Yes!" said Audrey, "I asked Brad if he thought you were nervous."

"Nervous about what?"

"Oh, about taking music lessons from Mr. Vaughan-Williams."

"Oh, a little, perhaps. But his letter made him sound so kind, and Reverend Wesley said he had heard he was a very gentle man. I'd say I'm excited about studying with him, because I think there is so much I can learn."

"While you're in the piano class, we'll check on Deputy Black, go to the library, and the *Denver Tribune* Office, and then see the sheriff," said Brad, listing their planned activities.

"Well," said their mother, looking at the clock on the wall, "I've got to be going. Look both ways when you cross the street; there are lots of horses and wagons. Denver is a busy city; it's not quiet like Riverton."

"We will, Ma," said Audrey.

Brad and Audrey watched their mother leave the hotel cafe and walk down the street. "We'd best tell Sheriff Strong about that man," said Brad.

"After we see Dan Black," said his sister. "We can do it this afternoon when we see him again about the robbery."

Brad and Audrey left the hotel and boarded a horse-drawn streetcar with a Franklin Street sign on the side. As they rode along, they watched a constant stream of wagons, buckboards, and men on horseback. Wagons entered alleys to make deliveries to the stores, while buckboards stopped in front where customers loaded their purchases.

"It's a little quieter on this side street," said Brad, after the streetcar made a turn.

"Yes, it is. I've been thinking about that man," said Audrey thoughtfully. "I could remind him of someone. Just because he looked at me doesn't really mean anything."

"You're probably right," he agreed. "And we won't meet Sheriff Strong until this afternoon, so there's no rush."

Several minutes later, they got off the streetcar and entered St. Joseph Hospital. They told the nun at the reception desk that they wanted to see Deputy Black.

"You must be Brad and Audrey Benton," she said.

"Yes, ma'am," replied Brad.

"Go right on in, he's expecting you."

"Brad, Audrey," said Deputy Black. "I'm glad you could make it. I told Mother Superior that I was expecting you this morning, and to please let you come in, even if you are under age for visitors."

"We took the Franklin Street streetcar, and it stopped right in front of the hospital," said Audrey. "Jim Bates told us about streetcars, and, well, now we've actually been on one."

"They have them back east and in California, too," he said. "San Francisco has cable cars, a streetcar that is pulled by a moving cable that lies under the street."

"Cable car?" said Brad, a quizzical look on his face.

"Yes, San Francisco has some very steep hills, which are hard on the horses, so they move the cars with cables under the street instead of horses."

They continued to chat until a nurse appeared and told them it was time to leave.

"Get your rest," encouraged Brad. "We'll be back tomorrow."

"Audrey, please stop and see Virgil Collins. He asked to see you again. Jesse Rebhorn is another story. He has a really bad case of lockjaw. He won't say anything other than to thank the nuns for his medical care and meals."

"I wonder what he wants," said Audrey as they left the room. A moment later they stopped at Virgil Collin's open door. Brad knocked on the doorjamb. Although he was handcuffed to the bed, the chain attached to the handcuff was long enough to permit him to rest his arm on his forehead. He moved his arm when he heard the knock and saw Brad and Audrey, smiled, and invited them in.

"Thank you for coming. The nurse said she'd tell the deputy that I wanted to see you."

"You look better than you did last night," remarked Audrey. "And a lot better than you did lying in the street yesterday afternoon."

"Thanks to your quick action. And, well, I don't know what to call it, so I'll just say thanks again for saving my life and also for saving my soul. I talked to the priest yesterday; told him what you had said about Christians. He told me about Jesus, the Catholic Church, and forgiveness. Well, I told him about the robbery, and other bad things I'd done. He said Jesus would forgive me, but that the government would still punish me."

"I'm very happy for you," replied Audrey. "Not about the punishment, but about your discovery of Christ."

"Me, too," said Brad.

"I know you're busy, and I'm a bank robber, but if you can stop in again, I'd really appreciate it."

"We're coming to see Deputy Black tomorrow," said Brad. "We'll stop and see you then. Good-bye."

Brad and Audrey entered the Denver Library and went to the librarian's desk. The librarian looked up from her work and in a soft voice said, "May I help you?"

"Yes," replied Brad. We're looking for information about Big Foot and about the Badger Gang."

"I see," she said, looking over the top of her glasses.

35

"Now, pray tell, why would you be interested in the Badger Gang?"

Brad and Audrey explained about their father being taken by Duke Badger, and their capture of one of the gang members.

"Well, this is a real pleasure," she exclaimed softly, standing up and grasping Brad's hand, and then Audrey's. "My name is Marion Carter, I'm the head librarian. I read the story about Duke Badger's death and the capture of some of the gang members. Was Marshal Benton a relative of yours?"

"Yes," said Audrey, "he's our uncle.

A discussion ensued and Brad and Audrey told her what their Uncle Henry had told them about Duke Badger's death, the capture of the gang members, and the rescue of Sarah Davis and Blue Bird.

"Well, you can start with those newspapers," said Mrs. Carter, showing them a stack in a large bookcase. "This is not a public library; membership is required, or users must pay a fee. But since you were a victim of Duke Badger, I'll waive the fee."

"Thank you," said Audrey, "we appreciate that."

Brad and Audrey skimmed the newspapers for articles about Duke Badger and Big Foot. Each time they found one, they'd stop, read it, and talk softly about it. After a few hours, they'd finished going through the stack of newspapers.

"Brad," whispered Audrey, "that stranger has been watching me again; he's leaving the library now. He's been watching us look through the newspapers."

"It has to be a coincidence," said Brad. "He wasn't on the streetcar, and we've been here a couple of hours."

"You're probably right, but he makes me uncomfortable."

"Probably because he has such a large head," Brad smirked.

"His head is quite large; that must be the reason." Audrey looked at her brother who was now suppressing a smile. "Brad Benton!" she whispered.

Brad and Audrey thanked Mrs. Carter, left the library, and started talking about lunch. A few minutes later they reached Wong's Cafe. Looking around, they selected a table against the wall.

"Sheriff Strong said the food was good," said Brad.

"He also said it wasn't a fancy place, and it isn't," his sister smiled.

A young Chinese girl came to their table and placed two glasses of cold water in front of them. Then, in excellent English said, "We have chili and cornbread, chicken soup and sourdough bread, and beef stew. Which would you like?"

"I'll take the chicken soup," said Audrey.

The girl looked at Brad. Brad blushed and said, "Sheriff Strong said your chili is great, so I'd like the chili and cornbread."

"I'll bring a chicken soup and a Sheriff Strong special," she said smiling at Brad. "The sheriff almost always has the chili and cornbread."

As soon as she left, Audrey leaned toward her brother, placed her hand on his arm, and whispered, "Brad Benton, you blushed. I do believe you like her. Am I right?"

"Yes. She's very pretty, and nice, and well, I don't know what it is, but, well, she's different, and I, uh,

37

felt sort of strange, well, a nice strange when she took our order."

"She is a nice girl, but you're going to meet many nice young ladies," predicted Audrey. "When she brings our lunch, look right at her nose or forehead, and say 'Thank you,' but do not look at her eyes. That should help you control your feelings."

"It can't be love," whispered Brad. "I'm too young for that stuff."

"You're not too young to notice a pretty girl; even though we're both too young to get married," said his sister. "And, we're not too young to feel love."

The young girl returned with their lunch, and said, "One chicken soup and one Sheriff Strong special. Is there anything else you need?" She looked right at Brad when she asked the question.

Audrey quickly responded, saving her brother from being enchanted by the girl's eyes, "I have a question." The girl turned toward Audrey, looking at her expectantly. "Could you tell me your name? My Ma collects names of girls, and I'd like to tell her yours, since I don't expect it is a name common in the United States."

"Sae-Jin," she said with a smile. "S, a, e, dash, J, i, n."

"Thank you," said Audrey, writing the name in a small notebook.

"You're welcome," said Sae-Jin, as she left to take a new customer's order.

"Brad, he just looked in the window at me."

"Who?" asked Brad, his eyes focused on Sae-Jin at the next table.

38

"The man that's been watching me."

"Where?" he said, suddenly attentive.

"He just looked in the window, then walked on down the boardwalk."

"We're going to tell Sheriff Strong about him," declared Brad. "He might know something."

They finished their meal, paid for it, and then left for the *Denver Tribune* office.

"This is it," said Brad, opening the door for his sister.

As they entered the newspaper office, they stood still for a few moments to let their eyes adjust from the bright sunlight. A man wearing a large apron, his shirt sleeves rolled up, was standing over a hand-operated printing press. He pulled a sheet of paper off the press, examined it, and looked up.

"May I help you?" he said.

"Yes," said Brad. "Marion Carter, at the library, said you may be able to help us. We're looking for information about the Badger Gang."

"Well, since she sent you, I believe I can. Follow me," and he turned and walked into another room. Brad and Audrey followed him.

"These are papers from other towns. I send them copies of my papers, and they send me copies of theirs. If I print an article from their paper, I give them credit; they do the same for me. You're free to look through the papers. Just keep them in order. I'll be at the press; I'm making a poster for the Percival Vaughan-Williams concert on June 16th."

"It will be a good concert," said Audrey confidently.

"How do you know about the concert? It hasn't been publicized yet."

"Our Ma is studying with Mr. Vaughan-Williams this week and next week," replied Brad.

"Well, she certainly has a good teacher. I'll be singing in his choir. We just call him Percival, Mr. Vaughan-Williams is a pretty long title."

"You resemble George Girard, who's the desk clerk at our hotel," said Brad. "He's singing in the choir, too. Are you related?"

"Yes, he's my brother. I'm David Girard."

"Marion Carter, the librarian is singing in the choir, too," said Brad.

"Well, the choir isn't too large," said Mr. Girard. "You've been fortunate enough to meet three of the members. I've got to get back to work. Let me know when you're done."

Brad and Audrey went through the stack of newspapers, finding several articles about the Badger Gang, their holdups, and the names of some of the gang members. When they finished, they went to David, who was still working the press.

"Mr. Girard, we found several articles about the Badger Gang. Do you know anything about the gang that hasn't been published?" asked Brad as he watched the newsman remove an announcement from the press.

"Not too much," he said, inserting a new sheet of paper in the press. "A number of men left his gang, primarily because he was such a mean tyrant."

"Nana calls him a despicable monster," said Brad, removing a newly printed poster from the press.

"Thanks," said Mr. Girard as he inked the type and inserted a fresh sheet of paper. "Your grandmother's

40

right. Duke Badger was a despicable, evil man. I don't know how he kept any men in his gang."

"He kept them through fear, intimidation, and greed," said Audrey. "His men were afraid of him, but they stayed for the easy money."

"What are you two planning to do while your Ma's studying with Percival?" asked David. "If you're interested, how about writing a short article about the Badger Gang? I'll publish it and include your names as authors. I can't pay much, though."

Brad and Audrey looked at each other, smiled and nodded in agreement. "We'd like that," replied Audrey. "We'll start writing tonight and bring you our draft in a few days, if that's all right with you?"

"Agreed. Just write on every other line of lined paper and leave wide margins. That will give me plenty of room to make my edits."

Their walk to the sheriff's office was slow and leisurely, but the excitement of writing for a newspaper was invigorating. The absence of their daily chores would provide ample time to write and do even more research on the Badger Gang, and Big Foot.

"I expect Sheriff Strong and Deputy Black know some things about the gang that haven't been printed in a newspaper," said Audrey.

"And writing about the Badger Gang is a lot safer than tracking them and capturing gang members," said Brad. "You won't even have to break the jaw of an outlaw."

"This will be a nice vacation," said Audrey. "I wonder what Sheriff Strong has learned since we talked to him yesterday."

They entered the sheriff's office and waited while he finished talking with a man wearing a suit. When the man left, Sheriff Strong waited until the door closed before acknowledging Brad and Audrey. "That was the owner of the bank that was robbed. I told him that we have no leads, and that Virgil Collins and Jesse Rebhorn refuse to identify the leader or any members of the gang."

"Thanks," said Audrey. "But I would like to tell you about a man that keeps looking at me."

"A man that looks at you doesn't sound unusual," remarked the sheriff. "There has to be more to that statement; am I correct?"

"Yes, he was at the hotel dining room last night, this morning during breakfast, at the library, and Wong's Cafe."

"Can you describe him?"

"Yes, I've even written down the description," said Audrey handing him a sheet of paper with a description and the times and places she had seen him.

The sheriff read what Audrey had written, looked up and said, "This is obviously more than a mere coincidence. I'll ask my deputies to quietly ask about a man fitting this description. They're pretty busy, so it will take several days. But I'll let Deputy Black know what I find out; I expect you'll keep visiting him."

"We will," confirmed Brad. "And if you have a few more minutes, we'd like to learn more about the Badger Gang. You see, David Girard at the *Denver Tribune* asked us to write an article about the gang. He'll include our names as authors and even pay us."

42

"He said he couldn't pay very much, but we'd like to do it," said Audrey.

"Well," replied the sheriff. I don't know much more than what has already been written. You two know more about the gang than I do. But, ask specific questions, and we'll find out what I know that you don't know."

Brad and Audrey asked numerous questions and learned a few additional pieces of information. When Brad told him about Audrey breaking Garth Pugh's jaw with her rifle barrel, the sheriff laughed.

"The other prisoners teased him about a girl breaking his jaw, really made life miserable for him," said Brad, standing up.

"That's good; he made life miserable for you and your father. Say hello to your mother for me," said the sheriff.

"We will," said Audrey. "We're going to meet her at the church now; her class is over at four-thirty."

"Stay together," cautioned the sheriff, "and let me know if that man appears again. Tell me about his horse, mannerisms, anything that might help me."

CHAPTER 5

"Well," said Brad. "We're at the church and no strange man."

"Yes," replied Audrey as they started up the steps, "but I still think he's watching me, it's happened too often to be a coincidence."

When they entered the sanctuary, they saw their mother and five other adults listening to Percival Vaughan-Williams. "Lift your hands at the end of a phrase. Lift them from the wrist and roll forward off the key. When you start a phrase, drop the hand with the fingers pointed down, this gives a strong tone and emphasizes the beginning of the phrase. The music you play must live; it must breathe. No two notes must be played exactly the same; they must be different, ever so slightly, in volume, in duration. The musical phrase must move forward, the same as a sentence spoken by an orator giving a speech. The orator does not speak in a monotone, and the musician should not play in a monotone. This concludes today's lesson. I'll see everyone tomorrow at nine. First thing tomorrow, I want each of you to play your piece for the class. Then we'll talk about your performance and how to make it better. You'll see how to make your music more exciting, how to bring it to life, how to make the

44

audience or congregation realize that they've really heard something special."

Mrs. Benton joined her children in the back of the church, and they went outside into the brilliant sunlight.

"It's such a beautiful day," said their mother. "Let's take our time and enjoy our walk back to the hotel."

"It is a lovely day," agreed Audrey.

"And a lovely day for a walk together," said Brad.

"Ma, you do have your .32 in your purse, don't you?" asked Audrey.

"Why, yes, I do. Why do you ask?"

"Oh, we were telling Sheriff Strong about you hitting all the pinecones last fall," said Brad.

"And he asked if you still carried it in your purse," continued Audrey.

"I see," said their mother, closing her left eye, and tilting her head as she looked at her daughter.

"Ma, we're not going to borrow it and hunt for the bank robbers," laughed Brad.

"I should hope not," half-closing her eyes as she looked at her son. "Sheriff Strong doesn't need your help; he has quite a few deputies for that."

"We're going to write an article about the Badger Bang," said Audrey changing the subject. "Mr. Girard, at the *Denver Tribune*, said he'd include our names as authors and pay us for it."

"It won't be a lot of money, Ma," confirmed Brad. "But we can show our new teacher what we wrote when school starts this fall."

"She may even give us extra credit for it," predicted Audrey.

"She may do that, but she may not," replied their mother.

"Well, at least we can hope," said Audrey.

"Here's the hotel," said their mother cheerily, putting her hands on her children's shoulders. "Let's get ready for dinner at the Silver Platter."

Wednesday Evening 8 June, 1881: "I'll ask for a table," said Brad, quickly walking up to the maitre d'.

"Oh, Ma, look at this picture," said Audrey, taking her mother's hand.

While his sister was showing their mother the picture, Brad asked the maitre d' for a table.

Audrey watched her brother talking with the maitre d' and thought, *what is he talking about? He just has to ask for a table for three. Well, at least the maitre d' is smiling; maybe we'll get a good table. But I know my brother; he may be doing something else, like asking about the man with the large head.*

"He has a table for us now, Ma," reported Brad, gently touching his mother's and then his sister's arm.

As soon as they were seated, their waiter arrived and recited the menu, then waited expectantly.

"I'll have your green salad and quail," said their mother.

"I'll have the same," said Audrey.

"And for the young man?" asked the waiter, as he turned to Brad.

"I'll have the trout."

After the waiter left Audrey turned to her brother
46

and said, "I thought you would have had the drover's steak."

"I thought about it, but when you and Ma talked about the cheese on the trout last night, I just had to try it."

"But this is a different restaurant, they may not use that Italian cheese on trout," argued his sister.

"I feel adventurous. And the sheriff Strong special I had for lunch was quite filling."

As they talked about their day, Abby described what she had learned, and Brad and Audrey told her about their trip to the library and the newspaper office.

The waiter arrived, served their dinner, and left. Brad looked at his trout. Then, sensing his sister looking at him, looked up.

"Well?" she asked.

Brad slowly chewed the fish, savoring the blend of flavors. "Yes, it does have that Italian cheese on it," answered Brad. "And, I saved room for dessert, too."

"I don't think you'll get a double dessert tonight," teased Audrey. "Last night was an exception. You won't be that lucky two nights in a row."

"I'm sure you're right," agreed Brad. "But it is nice to hope."

"Brad," whispered Audrey in her brother's ear. "That man, he just looked in the door of the restaurant, right at me."

"First thing tomorrow, we're going to see Sheriff Strong again," whispered Brad back. "I'm going to ask him to help us get a couple of pistols."

"What are you two whispering about now?" asked their mother.

"Another young lady," offered Audrey.

"Well, she is pretty," agreed Brad, picking up on his sister's cue.

"Yes, she is pretty," confirmed Audrey. "But let me tell you what I heard when I went to the ladies' room. I heard some women talking about the Silver Platter's marvelous pecan pie," deftly changing the topic from girls, much to Brad's relief, as the waiter approached their table.

"May I suggest our pecan pie?" said the waiter.

"A very small piece," said their mother.

"I'll have a piece, too," said Audrey. "I heard that it is marvelous."

"Harry, at the Denver Hotel, said to tell you he can go fishing Sunday," said Brad. "And he also told me that your pecan pie was his favorite. I'll take a slice, too."

The waiter smiled and left while Audrey slowly turned toward her brother.

"What - was - that – message – about - fishing – this - Sunday?" Audrey asked, speaking very slowly and precisely.

"Yes, please explain," said his mother sternly, clasping her hands together as she looked directly at her son.

"I met Harry this afternoon; he was our waiter last night. I told him that we were coming to the Silver Platter for dinner tonight. He said I must try the pecan pie, and he also told me to request Adonno as our waiter, which I did."

"But what about the fishing?" asked his mother,

who turned to look at her daughter who was stifling a laugh with her hand.

"He asked me to tell him that he could go fishing Sunday, so I did."

"Dessert for the Bentons," announced Adonno. "A small slice for Mrs. Benton."

"Thank you," said Abby.

"And a slice for the young lady," he said, placing a dessert plate with a slice of pecan pie in front of Audrey.

"Thank you," said Audrey.

"And two slices for Master Benton. One is broken so it couldn't be sold, but I told the chef that you knew Harry at the Denver Hotel, and wouldn't mind."

"Thank you," replied Brad. "And, no, I don't mind."

"Brad Benton!" exclaimed his sister. "I don't believe it, a double dessert, two nights in a row."

"It must be the old Benton charm," claimed Brad, happily digging in.

"Well, don't expect it to happen again," predicted his mother.

"It won't. This has to be a complete coincidence, like lighting striking twice in the same place."

The three Bentons entered the hotel lobby. Brad was the first to see Nurse Christine McLean sitting in a lobby chair reading *Harper's Magazine.* Before Brad could tell his mother and sister, however, Nurse McLean stood up and came to them.

"Abby, Audrey, Brad," she said, stopping next to them.

"Have you been waiting long?" asked Mrs. Benton.

"No, only a few minutes."

"We just had dinner at the Silver Platter. Your description of the food was exactly what we found. Marvelous food and excellent service," said their mother.

"Yes, I'm glad we went," said Audrey.

"The pecan pie was even better than your description," added Brad.

"All two pieces," chided Audrey, as she gently prodded her brother with her elbow.

"I'm glad you liked it. I've eaten there several times, and the food has always been marvelous."

"The hotel's German chocolate cake is very good, too," Brad noted.

"There are a number of good places to eat," said Christine. "Have you tried Wong's Cafe?"

"Yes," said Audrey. "Brad really liked the Sheriff Strong special."

"Maybe we can go there for dinner tomorrow," suggested their mother. "But It's time to get some rest. I never thought Mr. Vaughan-Williams' class could be so tiring."

"I'm working at the hospital tomorrow morning. I'll see you when you stop by to visit Deputy Black."

They talked in the lobby for a few minutes before the Bentons went up the stairs. As they climbed the stairs, they heard Nurse McLean asking the desk clerk when the next streetcar was due.

"I'll check the room, Ma," said Brad, unlocking the door. As he started to light the lamp, he heard a scream, felt a sharp pain on the side of his head, then blackness.

"You're coming with me, Nursie," ordered a large

man, clapping his hand across Audrey's mouth and nose with his left hand as he roughly shoved Mrs. Benton on top of her son.

Audrey fought, but the strength of the man was overpowering. She was half-carried half-dragged to an open window at the end of the hall. She tried to remove the man's hand but couldn't. He was too strong.

Mrs. Benton quickly struggled to her feet, opened her purse, removed her .32 revolver, and ran to the door yelling for help. The man had already shoved Audrey through the window to a waiting accomplice and was climbing out. Abby continued to shout, brought the .32 up, held it with both hands, aimed, and fired. There was a scream of pain from the man as he disappeared from sight.

"Bring my daughter back, you beast!" she screamed, running towards the window.

CHAPTER 6

Wednesday Night, 8 June 1881: Audrey found herself quickly tied, gagged, and blindfolded. The man who had kidnapped her from the hotel room whispered, "Quiet, little lady, and you won't be hurt."

"And if you're real smart, you'll remember that," laughed another man softly. "We're going for a buggy ride, then you get to ride a horse. I hope you know how to ride."

"Brad!" cried his mother, bending over her son, tears streaming down her face. "You need to wake up! Your sister's just been kidnapped!"

"Kidnapped?" questioned a man's voice behind her.

"That's right," she said, turning to the voice, her hands holding her son's head.

"I'm Karl Braunsohn, and this is Earl Martin. We're with the Pinkerton Detective Agency. Perhaps we can help. Our room is down the hall. We heard a shot and your screams. What happened?"

"When I opened the door, a large man hit my son, grabbed my daughter, and then shoved me down. I opened my purse, grabbed my pistol, screamed, and ran to the hall. The man was just about out the window, and, well, I shot that vile monster. I know I hit him because he screamed."

"Abby! Brad!" exclaimed Nurse McLean rushing toward them. "What happened? I heard screams and a shot."

Abby retold the story for Christine while the two Pinkertons examined the window at the end of the hall. Christine wet a towel in the water basin and placed it on the lump on the side of Brad's head. Brad's eyes briefly opened, then closed again.

"He's starting to come around," observed the nurse.

"Ooooohh, that hurts," groaned Brad.

"Just stay still for a bit," ordered Nurse McLean. "You took quite a blow. It looks like the kidnapper used his fist, which is good; otherwise you could be in pretty bad shape."

"Kidnapper," repeated Brad, still in the stupor of semi-consciousness, his eyelids fluttering as he strove to keep them open.

"Yes," said his mother. "Your sister was just kidnapped."

The two Pinkertons entered the room, and Karl asked, "Where did you learn to shoot, ma'am? It's about forty feet from your door to the window. And yes, you hit him. There's blood on the window sill and outside on the balcony, too."

"You shot the kidnapper, Ma?" asked Brad, groggily.

"Yes," her voice harsh with emotion. "But, unfortunately, I didn't kill him. He managed to get away with your sister."

"We're sure he had some accomplices," said Mr. Braunsohn. "He probably had a buggy waiting down below. An accomplice was most likely on the balcony, where they gagged your daughter, slid down a rope with her, put her in the buggy, and made their escape."

"I'll find her, Ma," said Brad, his voice sounding a little stronger. "We tracked Duke Badger and found Pa. I'll track down the kidnappers and bring her back."

"You're one of the young folks that tracked the Badger Gang and rescued their father in that blizzard last year?" asked Pinkerton Braunsohn.

"Yes, he is," said Mrs. Benton proudly, a tear streaking down her face. "But now with his sister gone, it's just Brad."

"With your permission, ma'am, we'd like to help your son find his sister," said Karl.

"I'd really like their help, Ma," said Brad, looking up at the Pinkertons. "I can't find Audrey alone, Sheriff Strong is already down one deputy, and he's trying to find the bank robbers."

"Of course, you have my permission to help my son," she said. "Are you aware that their father and I call them our Pinkertons?"

"No, ma'am," replied Detective Martin. "But that's a real compliment, coming from you."

"There's a shortage of doctors and nurses in Denver," stated the Pinkerton. "Someone probably saw your daughter taking care of the wounded in front of the bank yesterday. The word is around town about her nursing skills, your son's too. Your daughter was probably kidnapped to nurse someone."

"Why didn't they take me, too?" challenged Brad, who was now sitting up against the wall.

"Because the men that kidnapped your sister were

probably told to just get her," explained Pinkerton Braunsohn. "They dutifully obeyed that order and kidnapped your sister."

Audrey sat in the buggy beside Rex Reed, one of her kidnappers, who was complaining about the bullet in his arm. Audrey thought, *Good shot, Ma. And thanks, Pa, for teaching Ma how to shoot and for getting her the pistol.*

"I don't know how that woman did it," he said. "She shot the length of the hall and hit me. I've seen men stand 10 feet apart and empty their six-shooters, .45s, at each other and never get hit. She fired one shot and got me. She must be some kind of Annie Oakley."

The buggy left the road, and after several rather bumpy minutes they stopped. Audrey heard the driver climb down and talk with someone.

The driver returned to the buggy and informed Audrey, "We'll travel by horseback for a while now. I hope you know how to ride; if you don't, you'll learn mighty fast."

The kidnapper, Curt Bender, helped Audrey out of the buggy and removed her gag and blindfold. It was still dark, but she could see four horses picketed nearby. He handed her a canteen and said, "I expect you'd like some water, young lady, freshen up your mouth from that bandana."

"Yes. Thank you." Audrey took a drink, swished it around her mouth, and then spit it out. A second drink helped satiate her thirst.

"What's your name? asked Audrey.

"Curt Bender, but just call me Curt."

Audrey took another drink of water, but still held the canteen.

"Easy on the water, young lady," he advised. "We have several hours of riding ahead of us, and that's got to last."

A man adjusted the stirrups on a horse and brought it toward her. Audrey fought back a rising fear in her stomach as she realized that the man leading the horse toward her was the same man that had been watching her in Denver. The man had a large head.

"Up you go, little lady," said Curt Bender. "I'm tying you to your horse, but I'll leave your hands free. You won't be able to do much, since your reins will be tied to my horse, and Rex will be behind you. Any questions?"

"Yes!" she spat back. "Why have you kidnapped me?"

"I'm sorry, ma'am, I thought you knew. You'll be nursing some wounded men. The medical supplies are waiting for you."

Curt Bender, Rex Reed and the man with the large head mounted their horses, and the ride started. As they rode, Audrey remembered what Running Bear had taught her about tracking, and she began leaving clues. She decided to strip leaves from branches that were hanging down beside the trail.

By the light of the moon, Audrey could see the trees, branches, and brush on the abandoned trail. She looked around and thought: *I wonder how well trained this horse is. If she was used by a cowboy, she's probably very responsive to neck reining and pressure from a rider's knees. Well, there's one way to find out.* She gently pulled the horse's mane to the right and

56

applied knee pressure at the same time. The horse slowly moved to the right side of the trail.

Success, she thought. *If Brad tries to find me, I have to keep leaving him clues.* Audrey continued stripping leaves on some of the small tree branches that intruded onto the abandoned wagon road.

She looked at the men on the trail ahead of her. *I mustn't strip too much, or they'll notice. I'll count to thirty before I strip another tree branch.* When the horse moved back to the center of the trail, she again gently pulled its mane. Responding to Audrey's pull on its mane and her knee pressure, the horse again dutifully moved to the right side of the trail. Audrey stripped some leaves off and started her count to thirty. While she counted, the horse slowly moved back to the center of the trail. She repeated this process as they rode down the trail.

"How much further?" she asked.

"We're about half-way there," replied Curt Bender.

Audrey changed her clues. She started stripping just half the leaves off the branches, a silent clue to her brother.   She closed her eyes and said a silent prayer: *Lord, please guide Brad to my clues so he can find me. Please protect him and help him rescue me from these men.*

Audrey began to doze off, but woke when a branch brushed her face. She didn't know how long it had been since Curt had said they were half-way there. She started stripping leaves again. She calculated it had been about an hour when she heard Curt Bender say, "The ranch house is just ahead. It's on the other side of that meadow up ahead."

Again, she pulled the horse's mane to the right, and

quickly started to break branches, but not stripping the leaves. She continued breaking branches as quietly as she could, all the way to the clearing with the ranch house. As they entered the clearing, she thought, *Brad, I hope you see and understand the warnings I've given you.*

When they arrived at the ranch house, the men tied the horses to the hitching rail. Next, they untied the ropes holding Audrey's feet under her horse and helped her down. A man she recognized as Jake Rawlins came out of the house. He stomped toward her and snarled, "You're a nurse; there're wounded men inside that need your help. Get to work."

Curt Bender led her inside, picked up a black bag, and said, "Here's the doctor's bag, miss. You can start with Clete. I'll introduced you to the men as we go. Please cut formalities and call us by our first names. As I said before, call me Curt."

Clete Corbin was helped onto the kitchen table. His shirt had been removed and a crude bandage covered the wound in his side. Audrey exposed the wound, daubed the area with a solution of carbolic acid, picked up the forceps, and started prodding for the bullet. Clete groaned in pain, clenched his teeth, and waited for Audrey to finish.

When she finally removed the slug, he gasped, and then looked at her. Blinking in disbelief, he said, "Aren't you the young lady that was helping Virgil at the bank?"

"Yes."

"Then you saw who shot me?"

"Yes, I did. It was a bank customer that shot you

58

because you were shooting at me. What did you expect the man to do, not shoot at you? You had just robbed a bank and then you start shooting at an unarmed person tending to the wounded."

"That was my fault. I was scared; I shouldn't have shot at you. I'd like to call you something other than miss. Do you have a name?"

"Audrey."

"Audrey," replied Clete, as if savoring the name. "Thank you, Miss Audrey. Thank you for your doctoring."

Two of the men helped Clete off the table. "Chite is next," said Curt.

The two men lifted Chite Hobbs onto the table, brought the lamps closer, and looked at Audrey expectantly. Removing the bandages, she saw that the wound was festered and a sweet, sickening order caused her to instinctively back up. She dropped the small cloth that Curt handed her into the pot of hot water. Using the forceps, she picked up the dripping cloth and cleaned the pus off the wound. Chite gasped in pain as the hot cloth cleansed the angry red hole in his side.

"This is really going to hurt now," she said. "I'm going to apply a solution of carbolic acid to slow the infection." Audrey took a deep breath and daubed the area with the carbolic acid solution. The man gasped at the sudden pain.

"Let me give you some laudanum," advised Audrey. "You're going to need it when I start probing for the slug."

Chite gave a slight nod of agreement and waited for the medicine. Audrey poured some of the painkiller into an empty shot glass that still reeked of whiskey

59

and held it to his lips. He drank it with a couple of swallows.

"Are you starting to feel sleepy?" she asked a few minutes later.

Chite nodded, his eyes rolled back, and his body relaxed.

"He looks out to me, ma'am," observed Rex Reed.

Again, Audrey dipped the rag in hot water and this time wiped away the pus inside the wound. Then she dipped the forceps into the pot of boiling water, daubed the cleaned area with carbolic acid again, and then renewed probing for the slug. She worked in silence. Kidnapper Reed held the lantern with his good arm while Audrey tried, unsuccessfully, to find the slug. Some time later, she laid the forceps down and stepped back from the man.

"I'm sorry," she said. "I'm not a doctor. He needs a real doctor to find the slug. The wound is festering, and it's going to get worse. The slug and the piece of his clothing that the slug pulled into his body have to be removed. If they're not removed, the wound will not heal, it will only get worse. Without a doctor, he will probably die."

"You did your best, lady; I know you're not a doctor, but you're very skilled," sighed Rex Reed. "I also know you're tired and hungry. Do you want some food now, or after you treat the other wounded men?"

"Let me treat the others now; I'll eat later."

"That will be Clay," said Rex Reed. With the help of a heavy stick, he struggled to the table and lay down. Rex Reed helped him pull his trousers down to expose the wounded thigh, while Clay covered the rest of his body with a shirt.

"He's ready, Miss Audrey," said Rex.

Audrey cleaned the wound with hot water, then daubed the area with carbolic acid. "This is going to hurt," she said as she picked up the forceps.

Clay clenched his jaw, and tears flooded his eyes as Audrey probed for the lead slug. Clay's face was pale when Audrey finally removed the piece of lead.

"I still have to clean the wound and search for any piece of your trouser fabric that may be in the wound." Clay nodded to acknowledge what Audrey had told him.

Once again, Audrey washed the wound with hot water and, using a pair of tweezers, searched for the small piece of cloth. "I have it," she said holding up a small scrap of bloody cloth to show Clay. But Clay couldn't see it; he had passed out.

"Raise his feet," ordered Audrey. "We need to get blood to his head.

Rex called Turk Atkins over to help him and they placed some blankets under Clay's feet while Audrey bandaged the wound.

The men moved Clay to a cot near Chite and the stove. Rex looked at Audrey, removed his jacket and shirt, and then lay down on the table. Audrey quickly cleaned the wound, daubed it with the carbolic acid solution, removed the slug, and applied a bandage.

"A small wound, easy to clean. The slug was near the surface and I got the piece of shirt out, too. The cloth is what usually causes the festering and infection. Your arm will be sore for several weeks. It's important that you move your arm, flex it, use it. Don't chop wood but do be sure to use your arm. If you don't, you may never regain full use of it."

Audrey was given some cold venison, an apple, and a tin mug of water. When she finished, Turk Atkins took her upstairs, and led her to a small room with a bed. She looked around; daylight was just starting to come through the window. He closed the door, and she heard him lock it. Audrey lay on the smelly bed, closed her eyes, and immediately fell asleep.

CHAPTER 7

Thursday morning, 9 June 1881: Brad and his mother entered the sheriff's office. Sheriff Strong was standing at his desk, sorting through Wanted posters. Looking up, he saw the pained look on Abby's face and a hard, serious expression on Brad's.

"Mrs. Benton, Brad. I didn't expect to see you this early; where is Audrey?"

"My daughter was kidnapped last night," stated Mrs. Benton firmly. "I wounded one of the kidnappers. I only had time for one shot, or you'd be holding a hearing on the death of a man."

Brad and his mother told the entire story, concluding with the offer of the two Pinkertons to help in finding Audrey.

"You're very fortunate," said Sheriff Strong. "Karl Braunsohn and Earl Martin are excellent detectives. I wish they worked for me, but they don't. We've worked together on a number of cases and they've always found their man."

"Ma, I'll go back to the hotel and meet with the Pinkertons," said Brad. "Audrey would want you to continue your studies with Mr. Vaughan-Williams. Besides, there's nothing you can do except wait."

"I know, Brad, and I'm going to do just that. I'm going

to my class with Percival. The class will help me keep my mind off Audrey. I'll also talk to Father Thatcher about the kidnapping. Reverend Wesley knows him from Seminary."

"I'll see you later and tell you what we've found out," said Brad.

♘

As Brad entered the hotel, the doorman told him that the manager wanted to see him immediately. The desk clerk recognized him approaching the front desk, opened the manager's door, and announced, "Brad Benton is here, sir."

Brad entered as the manager was coming to meet him. "Mr. Benton, I'm shocked to learn about your sister's kidnapping. The hotel has hired two Pinkerton detectives to search for her. I'm sure they'll find her shortly."

"We've already started," said Detective Braunsohn, entering the office. "We need your help, too. Let's go into the restaurant and talk."

As they took their seats, the detective ordered two coffees, a pot of tea, and a small plate of pastries. As soon as they were alone, he said, "I wired your father and Sheriff Tate last night and told them about the kidnapping. Sheriff Tate said that your father was in St. Louis, but that he's expected back by the end of the week.

"Thank you," said Brad. "I wish Pa were here."

"Sheriff Tate also said that you were one of the best trackers in the area and that you would work with us, and that Reverend Wesley concurred. I know the

Reverend, from when he was one of Sheriff Strong's deputies. So my question to you is, what do you know about this kidnapping that you haven't told us?"

Brad was stunned for a moment, and then thought; *How do they know I haven't told them everything? Well, that must be why they're Pinkertons.*

"Well, Jake Rawlins led the gang that robbed the bank. Rawlins rode with Duke Badger, and although I have nothing to support my suspicions, I believe he's behind my sister's kidnapping."

Now the tables were turned, and the two Pinkertons were stunned. There was a brief silence as they thought about Brad's information. The detectives discussed the kidnapping as they finished their coffee, and Brad finished off the tea and pastry. The Pinkertons asked questions for a few more minutes as they finished the pastries and coffee.

I'm guessing we're going to be working together closely for a while. Call me Karl."

And I'm Earl," added Detective Martin.

"Let's go out back again and examine the alley with you," suggested Karl, standing up and heading for the kitchen. They walked past the stoves and preparation tables, opened the back door, and walked to the opposite side of the alley behind the hotel. "Earl and I were here first thing this morning. The buggy tracks are still visible, because the alley was wet last night with the runoff from Kim's Laundry. The buggy wheels are narrower than a wagon's, so the tracks are easy to see."

Brad looked up to the small balcony outside the hall

window. He saw the rope still tied to the railing and the buggy tracks, and understood what had happened.

"Whoever was in the kitchen last night, maybe one of the cooks, dishwashers, or waiters, saw something. Let's start in the kitchen," suggested Brad.

The Pinkertons started questioning the kitchen staff. Brad asked the manager for the names and addresses of those who had worked in the kitchen last night.

"Festus, a dishwasher, worked last night; he's due to arrive any time now," replied the manager. "He needs the money, so he works extra shifts several days a week. You'll recognize him; he's quite thin, bald, and has a short, scraggly white beard."

"Thanks," said Brad. "I'll look for him."

When Brad returned to the kitchen, he saw Festus, placed his hand on Karl's arm, and whispered, "That's Festus, we need to talk to him."

"Festus," said Detective Braunsohn, "The manager said you'd be in about now. We need to talk to you."

Festus looked at Karl, who he knew was a Pinkerton, and thought; *What does this lad and that detective want with me?*

"The hotel pays me to wash dishes, but I'm more than happy to be paid to talk."

Pinkerton Braunsohn smiled, opened the door to the alley, and said, "Let's go outside." Once outside, he continued, "Did you see anything unusual in the alley last night, such as men or wagons?"

Festus thought for a moment, "I did see a buggy here last night. It was parked there for quite a while, like it was waiting for someone."

"Did you recognize the driver?" asked Karl.

"No, just an average-looking man; nothing unusual about him. I just came out for a cup of coffee and some fresh air. It gets hot and steamy washing dishes, so I come outside when there's a lull in the work."

Karl nodded. "I understand. Was there anyone else in the general area that you wouldn't normally see?"

"Well, yes, there was a well-dressed man, nice suit, standing at the corner."

"What did he look like?"

"Nice suit, well-groomed like I said, and yes, there was one thing that caught my attention. He was rather tall, and he had a noticeably large round head."

Brad quickly looked at Karl, a shocked look on his face. Karl nodded and said, "Thank you, Festus. If you think of anything else, or hear something you think might be of interest to us, please tell the manager. And I ask that you not tell anyone what you've told us. If any of the kitchen staff ask you, tell them you told us that you didn't see anything. It is very important that you tell no one what you've told us, except the sheriff, of course."

"I understand," said Festus. "I know you're a Pinkerton detective, and I don't want any trouble. I'm working to build up my grubstake so I can go prospecting again. I know there's gold and silver out there just waiting to be found."

As soon as Festus returned to the kitchen, Brad said, "The man with the large head has been watching Audrey the last two days. We told Sheriff Strong about it yesterday."

"This may be an important piece of information," said Karl. "Tell me more."

Brad told him about the places and times that Audrey had seen the man watching her. When Brad finished, Karl nodded, then motioned towards the street.

The three of them walked down the alley, climbed onto the boardwalk in front of the hotel, and stopped. "Let's begin by checking the liveries for buggy rentals," said Karl. "We'll start with those closest to the hotel. Earl, take the liveries to the right. Brad and I'll start with those to our left. Come join us when you finish. In any case, we'll meet back at the hotel cafe at noon."

Earl started up the street to the first livery as Brad and Karl headed in the other direction. The first two liveries Brad and Karl visited didn't have buggies for rent. Karl pulled out his badge as they approached the owner of the third livery. "I'm Karl Braunsohn, Pinkerton Detective Agency. We're looking for a man that may have rented a buggy recently, probably late yesterday afternoon, early evening. It may still be out. I don't have much of a description, though."

"Pinkerton, you say. Nice-looking badge. My name's Skeets, owner of Skeets' Livery, the best livery in Denver. Most folks take horses, not buggies. But I have a buggy that is out right now; a gentleman by the name of Cornelius Calhoun rented it late yesterday afternoon. He left his horse, that large dun in the third stall. Real nice horse, pretty saddle, too. Said he'd be back around noon. His partner's horse is in the adjacent stall."

"Can you describe Mr. Calhoun?" said Karl.

"Sure can. He's a tall fellow, always dresses in a nice suit, and his head is large. I don't mean he thinks a lot of himself, I mean his head is large, probably has to get his hats custom-made."

68

Karl and Brad exchanged a knowing glance at each other. Brad looked in the stall and then said, "His horse sure is handsome; mind if I take a closer look?"

"No, you can look all you want, but nobody rides that horse but Mr. Calhoun."

"While we're here, I need to rent four saddle horses and one pack horse for a few days," said Karl. "It appears that you have enough available. Can I pick them out after lunch?"

"Sure," said Skeets, "but why wait. Let's pick 'em out now."

While Karl and Skeets talked, Brad picked up a horseshoe file and went to the stall with Calhoun's horse. "Easy, fellow," said Brad, soothingly, as he stroked the horse. "Let me check your hoof."

Brad firmly ran his hand down the horse's left rear leg and picked up the hoof. While holding the hoof, he used the corner of the horseshoe file to file a groove in the shoe. He stroked the horse again and left the stall. Looking around, he saw Karl and Skeets in the corral, still selecting horses. Brad entered the next stall with the horse belonging to Calhoun's partner. Brad talked calmly to the horse and filed a groove in the horse's right rear shoe. By the time he returned the file, Karl and Skeets were back in the barn.

"Mr. Calhoun's saddle sure is nice, Mr. Skeets," observed Brad as he examined the saddle, rubbing the leather. "Do you do his tack?"

"Sure do, that's why it's in such good shape."

"It feels so smooth and soft," said Brad, gently feeling the saddlebags and saddle. "They're in real nice condition." While Karl and Skeets selected another horse, Brad examined the saddle, opened a saddlebag, and looked inside. There were several fist-sized rocks and some small gold nuggets. Brad removed a rock and a small nugget and put them in his jacket pocket. Then he refastened the saddlebag and rejoined Karl and Skeets.

"Thank you for your time, Skeets," said Karl. "I must also ask that you keep our questions and discussion private. Please tell no one about our talk. We have many more liveries to visit, and we don't want to let the man we're investigating know that we're looking for him."

"You can count on me," said Skeets. "I've always cooperated with Sheriff Strong and you Pinkerton boys."

When they were back on the street, Brad said, "I think we've found our man."

"I think you're right, and now we have a name. I'll start an investigation of Mr. Calhoun," said Karl. "But we don't have much to go on."

"Yes, we do," said Brad, showing the rock and gold nugget to the Pinkerton. "I removed this from Mr. Calhoun's saddlebag."

"Now I know why your mother calls you a Pinkerton," laughed Karl. "That looks like an ore sample. Let's visit an assay office and then it will be time to meet Earl for lunch."

The assayer set the sample on the counter and said, "That sample probably came from the hills west of town. I've seen a lot of samples like that. There's enough gold in the sample to get a man's attention. But the yield is too low to make it profitable to mine. That doesn't mean that there's not a vein of high-grade ore there. What it does mean is that this sample came from a low-grade vein."

"Thank you for your time," said Karl.

When they were outside, the Pinkerton looked at his pocket watch and said, "Yup, its lunch time. Let's get back to the hotel and meet Earl. It's possible he's learned something, too."

"Roast beef sandwiches are what I recommend, men," said the waiter. "They come with half a large dill pickle, fresh from the barrel."

Brad nodded and Karl placed the order, "Three sandwiches and two coffees."

"And one lemonade," added Brad.

"I'll be right back with your order," replied the waiter.

"What did you find, Earl?" asked Karl.

"Nothing, what about you?"

Karl Braunsohn and Brad told him what they had found and showed him the ore sample.

"The livery is on the west side of the hotel, and the assayer said the ore sample was probably from the mountains west of town," said Karl. "So far, everything is pointing to the west side of town, but we still need more information."

"It does sound promising," agreed Detective Martin.

"I think the sheriff may be able to get some information while we follow the buggy tracks," said Detective Braunsohn. "Bring your rain slickers and warm clothes; we may be camping out tonight."

After lunch, Brad and the Pinkertons went to the

sheriff's office. "I'm glad you stopped in," said the sheriff. "Mrs. Benton was in a little earlier. As one would expect, she was very concerned about her daughter. Have you found out anything?"

"We may have," replied Karl, and he told the sheriff what they had discovered, including their decision to leave that afternoon to search for Audrey.

"I know some businessmen that have been very helpful in the past," said the sheriff. "If they don't have information about Mr. Calhoun, they'll be able to look for some without his hearing that I'm nosing around."

"Good. We'll get our horses and supplies and be on our way. The general store first," said Karl, striding out of the office and down the boardwalk.

At the general store, they bought bedrolls, food, canteens, cooking equipment, rope, and other essentials. After paying for the supplies, Karl asked the clerk to hold their purchases at the store until they returned with their horses later that afternoon. The owner agreed and said that they could load their horses in the alley behind the store.

"The gunsmith is next," said Karl. "Sheriff Tate said you're a good shot. Let's get a good rifle for you."

"I'd like the same make and model as the one at home," said Brad, as they entered the store. "I have a .38-40 1873 lever-action Winchester with a 24" round barrel. Its magazine holds 15 rounds."

"Do you have that model in stock?" Karl asked the gunsmith.

"I have several," he said, handing one to Brad. "I check and adjust the sights and test-fire every weapon in stock."

72

Brad handled the rifle and turned to Karl, "It's nice, and it feels just like mine."

"We'll take three," said Karl. "And three boxes of ammunition. That will give us 50 rounds per rifle. Add a box of .45 shells for our six-shooters, too."

"You want scabbards for the rifles?" asked the gunsmith.

"Yes," said Karl. "We'll be back in an hour for the guns. Is it okay if we come in through the alley?"

"Sure, I'll see you shortly."

CHAPTER 8

Thursday, early afternoon, 9 June 1881: Brad and his mother stood in the narthex of the church, tearfully embracing each other.

"Brad," said his mother softly, a tear trickling down her face. "I'm afraid. I don't want you to go, but I also know you're one of the best trackers in the state. If anyone can find your sister, it will be you."

"I'm afraid, too," confided Brad. "But Mr. Braunsohn and Mr. Martin are excellent detectives, and we've already found some leads. Sheriff Strong is checking out one of them. We also know that Jake Rawlins robbed the bank. I believe he kidnapped Audrey for her nursing skills and also to keep her from testifying that it was his gang that robbed the bank."

"It's time to be going," advised Karl, standing in the entry to the narthex. "We need your son to do the tracking, Mrs. Benton. If Sheriff Tate and Reverend Wesley hadn't said he was one of the best, we wouldn't be taking him. The fate of your daughter may rest with your son."

"I know," she said with determination, turning to look her son directly in the eyes. "Brad, go now, before I start bawling like a calf looking for its mother at a roundup."

Brad turned away from his mother and left the narthex with the two Pinkertons. Abby turned and slowly walked back into the sanctuary toward Mr. Vaughan-Williams' class.

"Mrs. Benton, could you join my wife and me in my office?" asked Father Thatcher.

"Yes," said Abby. "Thank you for making time for me." Tears were now streaming down her face as she followed the priest to his office.

"Mr. Calhoun returned the buggy about an hour ago," said Skeets.

"May we look at the buggy?" asked Karl.

"I thought you might want to do that," replied Skeets, a twinkle in his eye. "It's right over there. I have to clean it up, but I haven't touched it; I thought you'd want to look at it first."

"You know Pinkertons very well," grinned Karl, heading for the buggy. "Thank you."

The Pinkertons searched the outside of the buggy as Brad checked the inside. Detective Braunsohn spoke first, "Not even a cigarette butt. Anything inside?"

"Nothing so far," replied Brad, running his fingers between the seat and the backrest of the buggy. Then Brad stopped, pulled a small item out, and looked at it. "Eureka! I think we have something. This looks like a button from a woman's dress, possibly Audrey's dress." They continued searching the buggy for a few minutes, but found nothing else.

"Gentlemen," announced Karl, "It's time to pick up our horses."

"They're ready," confirmed Skeets. "I've already saddled them, my best saddles too. Only the best for you Pinkertons. You caught a thief several years ago, a dandy that mugged a couple of ladies. My son had been jailed by the sheriff. All evidence indicated that he was guilty."

"I remember that," said Karl. "He was your son?"

"Sure was, and still is," added Skeets. "But you caught the dandy that framed him and freed my son. So, only the best for you Pinkertons."

"Thank you," said Karl. "We appreciate that. Did you notice which way Calhoun went?"

"I thought you might ask that question, too," laughed Skeets, a grin on his face. "I followed them out of the livery and watched them ride away. They headed west, out of town, at a nice trot."

Brad and the Pinkertons went to the general store, loading their supplies in their saddlebags and on the packhorse.

"Now to the gunsmith," said Karl. "I don't think anyone has seen us with the horses. I want to keep it that way, too. Keep your hats low, and let's go separately to the gunsmith. We'll meet in the alley behind his store."

The three of them left the rear of the general store at one-minute intervals and took the alley to the gunsmith.

"Everything is all ready, gents," said the gunsmith as Detective Braunsohn paid for the rifles and ammunition. "Three rifles, three rifle scabbards, three boxes of rifle ammunition, and one box of .45 cartridges."

"Thank you," said Karl. "And if anyone asks you, you don't know anything about us."

"Whatever you say, Mr. Braunsohn."

They left the alley separately and took the road out of town heading west. Once out of town, they joined up and rode at a fast trot. As soon as they were past the farms, Karl reined to a stop. "Let's look for buggy tracks. The narrow wheels are distinctive, so it should be easy. It's the only clue we have to go on."

"We can also look for hoof marks with a groove," said Brad. "I filed a groove in the left rear hoof of Calhoun's horse and the right rear hoof of his partner's horse."

"You do think like a Pinkerton," chuckled Earl.

"Let's start looking for buggy tracks leaving the road as well as hoofprints with grooves," said Karl. "Brad, take the right side of the road; Earl and I'll take the left."

They walked their horses, looking intently at the ground for buggy tracks and hoofprints. At times, they dismounted and walked in front of their horses. After an hour of searching, Earl said, "It looks like someone left the road here. Brad, do these tracks look like the shoes you marked?"

Brad looked at the hoofprint, smiled, said, "Yes," and began examining the area around the marked hoofprint. "And here are some buggy tracks."

They followed the tracks, with Brad leading, some distance down an abandoned road. Brad raised his hand, stopped, dismounted, and tethered his horse to a small tree. Kneeling, he described what he saw to the Pinkertons.

"Here's where they parked the buggy. It looks like they unhitched the horse from the buggy and tethered it here overnight."

"Anything else?" asked Karl.

"I'm not sure, yet," said Brad, carefully examining the ground. "Yes! It's a woman's shoe print. It's small; it has to be Audrey's."

Brad showed the footprints to the Pinkertons, explaining what he had looked for, and what he would be looking for as they continued their search.

"They had some horses picketed over here," noted Earl, as the three of them searched the area. "And here are the remains of a small campfire; recent, too. I suspect someone was waiting here with horses for the men and your sister when they arrived in the buggy."

"Now the big question," said Brad. "Why did they switch from the buggy to horses? The road, although abandoned, looks good enough for a buggy."

"Let's find out," replied Karl, mounting his horse. "It's late in the afternoon, but there are still several hours of daylight left. That's enough daylight for some more tracking."

Brad and Earl mounted their horses and joined Karl. Brad led the way, stopping every so often, dismounting, and checking the hoofprints. They had been riding only about ten minutes when they found the road blocked with a rock slide.

"That's why they switched to horses," said Karl. "There's no way a buggy could travel around that slide, but it's not a problem for horses."

Brad stopped in front of a tree branch, examined it, and said, "Now I know Audrey was here. She stripped the leaves off the branch, but not the last two or three leaves. Most people would have stripped off the leaves through to the end of the branch; they wouldn't have stopped a few leaves from the end."

78

Half an hour later, Brad stopped again, and examined a branch that was half-stripped. "Were getting close, she only stripped half of the leaves."

They continued on, Brad commenting each time he saw a branch with stripped leaves.

"A new clue!" announced Brad. "Let's get off the trail."

"What is it?" asked Karl, heading down a small gully.

"I'm coming across broken branches, but no stripped leaves. I believe that Audrey is warning me, but I don't know why."

"Here's a good place," said Karl, selecting a small clearing well off the trail. "Earl, go ahead on foot and see what's ahead."

Earl took off his hat, checked his pistol and rifle, and then quietly moved into the forest. Brad and Karl tethered the horses and then settled in behind some bushes and a large boulder.

The sun was low in the sky when Earl returned. "There's a ranch house just over the hill, and a man with a rifle is watching the road."

"The man could be guarding a mine," suggested Karl.

"Or, he could be the lookout for the Rawlins Gang," said Brad.

"We can get the guard now, bypass the guard, or wait," said Karl. "Earl, Brad, what's your opinion?"

There was a brief discussion of the merits of each action and the possible outcomes. Karl announced his decision. "We'll wait."

CHAPTER 9

Thursday evening, 9 June 1881: Brad and the two Pinkertons rode back up the abandoned road about a mile and made camp. They selected a site off of the road behind a small hill with a nearby creek.

"We'll build a simple lean-to," said Karl. "Earl, you take care of the fire and the small branches for the bedding. Brad and I will build the lean-to. It just might rain, maybe even sleet. There's no way of knowing."

Later that evening, the three of them were leaning back on their saddles, their feet pointing toward the dying campfire. The evening meal had been completed, dishes cleaned, and the Pinkertons were enjoying their last cup of coffee. Brad sat on his haunches, his elbows on his knees and his head cupped in his hands. Thinking about how to rescue his sister, he was oblivious of the Pinkertons and his surroundings.

"Brad," said Karl poking him. "I called your name several times, but you didn't hear me. You must be deep in thought. What are you thinking?"

Before he replied, Brad looked at one Pinkerton, then the other. "I think we ought to scout out the ranch tonight. There's just enough moonlight to see by, and if we're careful, too little to let us be seen by the lookout."

"It would give us a better feel for what we're up

against," agreed Detective Martin. "The boy and I have good night vision, and we need someone to stay with the horses. It'll be just like we did on that case in Montana last year."

Karl Braunsohn smiled and replied, "You're right, let's do it."

Brad looked at the Detective Braunsohn and then said, "Case in Montana?"

"My night vision is poor," he explained. "On the Montana case I stayed with the horses one night while Earl checked out a thief's campsite."

"And did you capture him?" asked Brad.

"He's in prison now," replied Detective Martin. "We also recovered most of the money he'd stolen, which we returned to the railroad. But enough of that," he said, standing up. "If we leave now, we should be back before midnight."

They saddled their horses, kicked some dirt on the dying embers of the campfire, and mounted up. Earl took the lead, with Karl at the rear. They stopped about a quarter of a mile from the ranch house and tethered the horses in a very small clearing off of the road. Karl checked his pistol and burrowed into some nearby bushes.

"We'll whisper the password when we return," said Earl.

Brad took off his boots and placed them in his saddlebags, and slipped on a pair of moccasins. They nodded at each other and then crept away towards the ranch house. Karl watched them as the forest and the night quickly enveloped them in darkness.

When they reached the edge of a small corral behind

the barn, they stopped and watched for activity at the house. "There's a man on the porch," whispered Brad.

"I didn't see the lookout on the hill," said Earl softly.

"I didn't either," whispered Brad.

They studied the house. Brad commented, "There's a window on the second floor that's boarded over, like jail bars."

"Let's check the barn and corral," whispered Earl.

As they crept up to the corral, Brad sang a mindless tune very softly, as soft as a whisper, so the horses wouldn't get nervous and spook.

"Calhoun's horse is in the corral," said Brad. "Quite a few other horses there, too."

"I count about 10 horses," said Earl. "But they're moving and it's dark."

"It's time to tell Audrey that I'm here," said Brad, touching Earl's shoulder.

Earl grabbed Brad's arm, looking at him in disbelief. "You can't be serious; you could get us killed."

"Not that way," whispered Brad. "I'm going to do it like an Indian. I'll howl like a wolf. Everyone but Audrey and the horses will think it's either a wolf or some Indians."

"Let them think it's a wolf tonight," said Earl. "Tomorrow night, we'll let them think it's Indians."

Brad backed into the trees several feet, leaned back and a long howl of a timber wolf burst forth from his mouth. Earl looked and listened, not really believing what he had just heard. The horses knew, however, that it wasn't a real wolf and remained calm. Brad waited a few minutes, then howled again, softly. After another pause, he howled loudly again.

82

"Okay, let's go," said Brad. "Audrey knows I'm here."

Inside her room, Audrey heard the howl of the wolf, and sat up in the smelly bed on which she had been sleeping. She heard the guard snoring in the chair outside her door.

That was either a wolf, an Indian, or Brad, she thought. She looked at the moonlight streaming through the wooden bars on her window and waited. She heard what she thought was another wolf replying. And she waited. The wait seemed like an eternity, but she knew it was only a minute.

When she heard the wolf howl again, she had her answer, and thought, *that is Brad. He's found me. Thank you, Lord. Thank you.*

Brad and Earl crept back into the forest and started their return to Karl and the horses. Every few minutes they would stop, listen, and look at the house. They had just made one of their stops when they heard a scurry of a small animal that they had disturbed.

"Must have been a rabbit, or a squirrel," said Brad softly.

Suddenly a large bird flew silently over their heads, toward the ground behind them. Brad turned and saw the bird grab something in its talons, heard a short squeak, and they watched the bird fly away into the forest.

"Looks like an owl just got dinner," said Brad, as he and Earl resumed their trek.

When they reached the area where Karl and their horses were supposed to be, Brad stopped and softly said the password: "Audrey."

Karl replied, "Abby. Welcome back. Let's return to camp, then you can tell me what you saw."

They mounted their horses, and, with Earl in the lead, headed back to their camp. As predicted, it was around midnight when they dismounted. Brad built a small fire while Earl filled a pot with water from the creek. Before long the fire was going nicely and the water was steaming.

"We'll have tea, since it's so late," said Karl, getting the tin mugs ready.

When the water started boiling, Brad added a big pinch of tea and took the pot off the fire. Earl opened a saddlebag, pulled out a sack of oatmeal cookies, and passed them to Brad.

"Earl, your observations first," said Karl. "And Brad, how about pouring us some of that tea?"

"Three teas," replied Brad, pouring the hot tea into the mugs.

"We didn't see the lookout; he's probably only there during the day." Earl picked up a mug of tea and continued. "We watched the house for a while and saw a guard outside on the porch. There were quite a few horses in the corral, just waiting for some young Indian braves to prove their courage and raiding skills."

"Brad, what did you learn?" asked Karl, just before he bit into a cookie.

"There are about ten horses in the corral, and Calhoun's horse is one of them. A window to a second-floor room, probably a bedroom, is barred with boards. I believe Audrey is in that room."

"Anything else?" asked Karl.

"We prepared them for the Indians, too," said Brad.

"How did you prepare them for Indians?" asked Karl, taken aback by Brad's statement.

"Brad's wolf howl sounds like a real wolf," explained Earl. "It sent a shiver down my spine."

"That was you?

"Yes. I was telling Audrey we were here."

Karl looked at Earl for clarification. "You know how young folks are, Karl, secret codes and things. Remember the stripped leaves? Well, it seems that Brad can howl like a wolf, too."

"Despite the darkness, and my poor night vision, I think I see. Do you have any suggestions?"

"Someone is probably going to go into town tomorrow or the next day," predicted Brad. "Let's capture him and find out who's in the ranch house."

"And if no one leaves tomorrow, we can always stage an Indian raid and steal some horses," said Earl. "Make them nervous, lose sleep, start wearing them down. It'll let them know that they're not in charge, we are; but we won't let them know who we are."

Karl pondered these suggestions. "I like these ideas. Let's get some sleep and be ready to cause some real mischief tomorrow."

CHAPTER 10

Friday Morning, 10 June 1881: The sunlight came through the bars in the window, striking Audrey's face. She turned over to escape the light and remain in her sanctuary of sleep. The sanctuary didn't last long, however, as it was destroyed by a fist pounding on the door.

"Time to get up, little Nursie," shouted Turk Atkins, her door guard, through the door. "Some men need your doctoring."

Audrey sat up, and the memories of the kidnapping, long ride, and treatment of wounded men flooded into her consciousness. She immediately wondered, *Brad, was that really you last night, or just a dream?*

Turk unlocked her door, opened it a little, and said, "You're needed downstairs, miss. The boss gets mean if he's kept waiting. You'd better go right now."

Audrey stood up, rubbed the sleep from her eyes, and followed him downstairs.

"Good morning, Clete," greeted Audrey, as she removed his bandage. "How do you feel?"

"A mite better than yesterday. Your doctoring really helped."

"I'll clean the wound with hot water again, daub more carbolic acid on it, and apply a new bandage. It's

86

not festering; it appears to be healing nicely. Use this arm lightly for a week to allow time for the wound to heal."

"I'll do just what you say, Dr. Audrey," a pained smile on his face from the carbolic acid. He got off the table and watched as Rex replaced him.

"Rex Reed," said Audrey, removing his bandage. "I'm going to have to talk to my mother about you."

"Why?" asked Rex.

"She didn't shoot straight."

"Your mother is a great shot," said Rex. "She's a real Annie Oakley. I'm just glad she was out of sorts when she shot me, or I might not be here."

"That's why I have to talk to her. If she had been in sorts, I wouldn't be here, either," replied Audrey. "Tell me, who is this Annie Oakley you mentioned?"

"Annie Oakley is one of the best marksmen in the world. She hunts pheasants and quail with a rifle, not a shotgun; kills them with a shot to the head."

"That's right," confirmed Clete. "I saw her shoot in Cincinnati in 1875. She competed with Frank Butler, the famous marksman."

"I've heard about Frank Butler," said Audrey. "Pa told me about his shooting skills."

"Well, Annie Oakley beat Frank Butler in the competition," stated Clete.

"Frank married her the next year," added Rex. "Annie is a very petite lady, but a real giant when she has a rifle in her hands."

"What are you jawing about?" demanded Rawlins.

"We're just talking about what she's doing," replied Rex. "She's being a good doctor."

"Thank you," whispered Audrey, seeing the warning look in Rex's eyes.

Next, Clay Austin hobbled over to the table, and Audrey cleaned and re-bandaged his wound.

"It appears to be healing nicely. Walk slowly, and often, gradually walking faster and farther. You need to slowly increase the use of the leg. However, be careful going up and down steps. If you don't use your leg while it's healing, despite bearable pain, your leg may freeze up. If that happens, you'll be crippled for the rest of your life.

Chite Hobbs was in a bunk, his breathing labored. A couple of men moved him to the table. Audrey moved the lantern closer to his chest as she removed the bandage. The inflamed area around the gunshot wound was larger than last night, hot to the touch, and red streaks could be seen under the skin, emanating from the wound site.

"Let me clean your wound again," said Audrey.

"Thank you, Audrey," said Chite. "Thank you for helping me. I hurt something terrible. Am I going to make it? Tell me straight."

"Rex, please hold the lantern a little closer," said Audrey. "And Clete, please bring that other lantern, I need more light."

Rex and Clete held the lanterns close to the wound, shielding Audrey from Jake Rawlins. Audrey knelt beside Chite and said softly, "I don't think you're going to make it. I'm not even sure a real doctor could help you now. If a doctor had treated you a couple of days ago, you might have made it, but not now. The infection is spreading; there's nothing I can do except give you more laudanum to relieve the pain."

"How long do I have?" asked Chite.

"Less than a day," replied Audrey, her voice choking. "Doc Adams told me about this kind of wound. You need to say goodbye to your friends and make peace with the Lord."

"We're bank robbers," whispered Chite. "We're not churching men. We've spent our lives robbing, stealing, and even killing. The Lord won't be wanting to make any peace with me."

"If you sincerely ask for forgiveness, he'll forgive you. May I lead you in prayer?" she asked.

"Please, Miss Audrey."

In the early light of dawn, aided by the yellow glow of the lanterns held by two wounded men, she took Chite's hand and whispered, "Please repeat after me, 'Lord, please forgive me.'"

"Lord, please forgive me," repeated Chite.

Lying on his deathbed, in a body rapidly being destroyed by infected gunshot wounds, Chite asked for forgiveness.

After the prayer, Audrey cleaned Chite's wound, daubed it again with a solution of carbolic acid, and prepared a clean bandage. After she finished bandaging him, Audrey said a silent prayer. Rex and Clete helped her stand up and whispered their thanks to her.

"Let me give you some more laudanum for the pain," said Audrey, her eyes puffy with sorrow.

"Thanks," said Chite. "Thanks for your doctoring," and he whispered, "and for your prayers." Then he grasped her arm, and pulling her close, he continued.

"Jake is not going to let you go. If you have a chance to escape, do it. You can trust Rex and Clete to help you."

A shiver of fear jolted through her, the shock of Chite's revelation obvious to the three men looking at her. Audrey looked at Rex Reed, who nodded in agreement, and then Clete Corbin, who also gave her a very slight nod.

"We'll help you when the chance comes, Miss Audrey," whispered Rex.

"You can trust us," added Clete. "Our lives depend on it."

It was around eight o'clock when Earl said a rider was coming. They took their pre-arranged positions as the rider drew near. Karl raised his rifle and stepped out in front of the oncoming rider. At the same time, Earl, with his rifle raised, came out of the bushes beside the rider.

"And I'm behind you, with my rifle aimed at your back," said Brad in his deepest voice.

The rider slowly raised his arms.

Karl walked forward, grasping the horse's reins with his left hand while keeping his rifle pointed at the rider with his right. "Now place both hands on the saddle horn and slowly dismount."

Brad disarmed the rider while the two Pinkertons covered him. Brad tied the man's hands and they took him to their camp, about a hundred feet away.

Karl asked the questions, while Earl studied the man.

"Like I said before, my name is Jade Wellman. I'm

a guard for the mine. We're going to re-open the mine next week. I'm part of the advance group."

"Now your boss's name wouldn't happen to be Jake Rawlins would it, Mr. Wellman?"

The shock of hearing his boss's name from complete strangers was too much for him; Jade's jaw fell open in disbelief.

"And I suppose you don't know anything about Tuesday's bank robbery, either," added Karl.

"How did you know about that?"

"We have determined your name and know you're a bank robber," replied Karl, ignoring Jade's question. "I believe you heard some wolves last night. Am I right?"

"Uh, right."

"Those were Indians, not wolves," explained Karl. "Now you can answer all of my questions, or I can let my Indian friends help me. What do you want to do?"

"You're a lawman; you won't turn me over to any Indians," stammered Jade.

"Well, I'm not a lawman," said Brad forcefully. "I won't hesitate to give you to the Indians. Further, that's my sister you have in the house. If you answer all of Karl's questions, I won't drag you to the Indians' camp. Make up your mind while I saddle my horse."

Brad turned, picked up a saddle blanket, and placed it on the back of his horse. He swung the saddle into place, tightened the cinch, and mounted his horse.

The prisoner looked at Karl, then Earl. "You're not serious," he squeaked. "You wouldn't turn me over to a kid to take to the Indians?"

"You're right that I wouldn't do that," replied Karl casually. "But Brad can and will. Once you're gone, no one will know except us. The choice is yours; better make up your mind fast."

Brad slowly turned the horse toward Jade, uncoiling a rope from his saddle. He tossed the end of it to Earl, who knotted the rope around Jade's hands. Brad tied the rope to his saddle horn, turned, and said, "Silence means no." He gave a soft cluck, his horse started forward, and Jade was instantly forced to either walk fast or be dragged behind the horse.

"Wait, I'll tell you everything," cried Jade.

"Whoa," said Brad, as he pulled back on the reins. He turned in the saddle and said, "Talk now. Next time I won't stop."

"I'll tell you everything," wailed Jade, his eyes wide in fear like a scared cow.

"Tell me about everyone in the house," said Karl.

"There's a girl, I think her name is Audrey. And there's Jake, he's the boss. Then there's Bobby Cole, and Turk Atkins. Turk's been guarding the girl. And there's Curt Bender and three wounded men. That's why we got the girl."

"Tell us about the wounded men," said Karl.

"Clay Austin, Clete Corbin, and Chite Hobbs, they were shot during the robbery. Chite is in pretty poor shape. The girl said he needed a real doctor or he might not make it. And then there's Rex Reed, he was wounded when they kidnapped the girl."

"Who owns the nice horse with the fancy saddle?" asked Earl.

"I don't know his name, but he has some kind of agreement with Jake."

"How's Audrey?" asked Earl.

"She's fine. The men like her, all except Jake. He doesn't like anybody. She did some fine doctoring on the men, even though she said she's not a doctor."

"Anything else you might have forgotten to tell us?" demanded Karl.

"I told you everything. Just don't let that kid drag me to the Indians."

"What questions should I have asked you that I didn't?" said Karl, with a wicked smile.

"Well," replied Jade. "The men got spooked about the wolves last night. Jake told them not to worry, that the wolves wouldn't bother them."

"Did the men believe him?"

"Not really. We've all heard stories about wolves attacking men."

"Yes," nodded Brad. "I've seen them surround a wounded man. My sister and I killed four of them just as they were getting ready to attack our Pa last fall."

Jade looked at Brad, a puzzled look on his face, then his eyes opened wide in disbelief, "You're the kids that tracked Duke Badger and rescued your father in that blizzard?"

"That's right," confirmed Karl. "Now you know what a mistake Jake Rawlins made when he kidnapped Audrey."

"Her brother tracked you, just like an Indian, right to the ranch house. We even visited your corral last night," said Earl.

"Tie him to a tree, and put a gag in his mouth," ordered Karl. "I don't want him talking to his partners when we bring them back."

CHAPTER 11

Midmorning, Friday, 10 June 1881: Brad and the two Pinkertons dismounted a half-mile from the house. Just as he had done twelve hours earlier, Brad removed his boots, placed them in his saddlebags, and slipped on his moccasins. The three slowly approached the lookout. Karl and Earl set themselves up to provide a good crossfire, if necessary, on the hapless man. Brad slowly crept forward; it took him nearly fifteen minutes to cover the last fifty feet. He moved slowly, stopping each time the man looked in his direction. When Brad was finally in place, he threw a rock into a small clump of bushes behind the lookout.

The lookout turned, trying to see whatever it was that had made the noise. Seeing nothing, he turned back to face the road. A minute later, Brad threw another rock into the bushes. Once more, the lookout turned, his eyes searching for the cause. This time, just as the man turned his attention back to the road, Brad threw a larger rock.

"All right!" The man, carefully approached the bushes, moving out of sight of the ranch house. "What's going on?"

"Quiet, now. Three rifles are pointed at you,"
94

instructed softly, standing up with his rifle pointed directly at the man's chest.

"Easy, son, you could kill a man with that thing."

"Don't worry about this gun, worry about the two behind you."

"That's right," said Karl.

The lookout dropped his rifle and slowly raised his hands.

"You learn quickly," said Earl.

The lookout was quickly gagged, hands tied, taken back to the picketed horses, and tied to a tree.

"Now for some good old-fashioned horse-thieving," said Karl, rubbing his hands in anticipation. "Let's go."

The three of them crept to the barn, quietly saddled all but two of the horses, tied a lead to all of them for a fast get-away, then led them into the forest.

"Now that we're ready to go, shall we quietly take another prisoner?" said Karl.

"Yes," said Brad.

There was a brief discussion about the prisoner to be. Karl led the way as Brad led the two horses without saddles back into the barn.

"Calhoun's horse isn't here," said Earl, looking around. "He probably departed after Jade left and took a different route back to Denver."

"We haven't seen the last of him. He'll show up again," predicted Karl.

"I found our distraction," said Brad, watching something move under a fallen tree.

Brad took a large sack from a peg on the side of the barn, opened it, and crept up to the fallen tree. He watched intently for a minute, then picked up a stick

95

and cut the branches so that he had a fork at one end. Kicking away some debris, he exposed a large black snake, which he pinned down with the forked stick. Grabbing the snake just behind its head, he stuffed it into the sack and closed the top.

"Let's go back to the barn," said Brad.

When they entered the barn, he opened the sack, and dumped the snake onto the barn floor in front of the two horses. Immediately, the horses were spooked, they whinnied and kicked the walls of the barn. In simple terms, they really raised a ruckus.

Rex Reed left his chair on the porch and headed to the barn. "Something is spooking those dumb critters," he muttered.

As soon as Rex entered, he saw the black snake on the floor. Hearing something, he turned, only to see Karl pointing a rifle at him.

Rex dropped his rifle and slowly raised his hands. Without saying anything, Brad removed Rex's gun belt, blindfolded him, and tied his hands.

"Do you have a name?" asked Brad.

"Rex, Rex Reed."

"Now I'll gag you, Rex."

Earl walked Rex out of the barn and into the woods where the horses were picketed. Brad talked soothingly to the two horses as he led them into the forest. After tying Rex securely to a tree, they started back to the barn.

"I think we're ready," said Karl as Brad and Earl entered the barn.

"Agreed," said Earl, looking at Brad.

Brad nodded in agreement, with a grim, but firm, look.

"Take my pistol, just in case," said Karl sternly, offering it to Brad.

"Thanks. But I don't think I could shoot a man, even those that kidnapped my sister."

"I know," said Earl. "But if they shoot at you, you'll need a gun to defend yourself and your sister."

"You're right," said Brad, taking the pistol and pulling his mother's .32 from his pocket. "Ma said that, too."

"You have a smart mother."

Brad turned just before he went into the forest and said, "I'll wave to you when I'm ready."

Fifteen minutes later, Brad had crept up on the blind side of the house, climbed a tree, lowered himself onto the porch roof, and crept up to the second-floor window. Peering into the hall window, he saw a guard leaning back in a chair in front of the door. He crept around the porch roof to the front of the house. When he reached the barred window, he looked in, saw his sister, and gently scratched the window frame.

What's that? thought Audrey. She looked at the window only to see her brother looking through the wooden bars with his finger across his lips. Audrey clasped her hands over her mouth to suppress a shout of joy. Brad pointed to the door, pointed at her bed, and mimed pushing and pulling it. Brad put his index fingers in his ears and then was gone. *He's got something cooking, and its probably outlaws. It appears he wants me to add some noise to his stew pot.*

Audrey pulled her bed away from the wall, then

pushed it across the room, and shrieked, "A mouse! Take that!" and stomped the floor. "And that!" as she stomped again. She shoved the bed across the floor into the wall and then jumped up onto a chair.

"What's going on in there?" demanded Turk.

"I'm chasing a mouse," she said excitedly. "I could use some help."

Turk unlocked the door and shoved the bed around the room but didn't see a mouse. Audrey got down from the chair, flipped the mattress, the blankets, and the pillow. No mouse appeared.

Meanwhile, Brad raised the window to the adjacent bedroom, climbed inside, crept across the floor, and opened the door to the hall. He heard the guard in his sister's room, and quietly shut the door again.

"Well," said Audrey, "You must have scared it away. Thank you."

Turk left Audrey's room and locked the door, leaving the key in the lock so Audrey couldn't look through the keyhole. As soon as things were quiet, Brad went to the window, waved, and thought: *Now the excitement will begin. Let's see how the Rawlins Gang likes it when they're shot at and their nurse disappears.*

Suddenly, a couple of shots rang out. Broken window glass flew across the front room of the ranch house. The men grabbed their rifles and pistols and hurried to the windows to return fire. The Pinkertons obliged and fired a few more rounds from the barn before running to the woods beside the barn to shoot again.

"There must be five or six of them, Jake!" yelled Curt. "They're in the barn and in the woods."

"Turk!" shouted Jake. "Get down here. Now!"

Turk ran down the stairs as he drew his six-shooter. Brad waited until Turk was down the stairs before quietly slipping down the hall to free his sister.

"Audrey! Take this," he whispered, handing his sister their mother's .32 pistol. "Take your shoes off. Hurry, we don't have much time."

Brad motioned his sister into the adjacent bedroom as he relocked her room. "I'll explain later. Go out the window. I'll be right behind you."

Audrey quickly went through the window and crouched against the side of the house. Brad climbed out the window, quietly shutting it behind them. While the gun battle raged below them, they crept along the porch roof on the front of the house and continued around the corner until they reached the tree. Brad helped his sister get a good grasp, watched her start down, then climbed down after her. As soon as he reached the ground, he grabbed her hand and they ran into the woods.

"Brad Benton!" Audrey exclaimed as soon as they were safe. "Were you baying at the moon last night?"

"Then you did hear me," he laughed, a big smile on his face.

"I thought it was you, but it sounded so real, I wasn't sure."

"I've got a couple of friends with me, Pinkertons," explained Brad. "They're in the barn. We have to hurry."

"Let me put on my shoes first."

As soon as her shoes were on, they left at a slow trot through the forest to the rear of the barn.

"It's about time," groused Karl when Brad and

Audrey arrived. "We didn't bring enough ammunition for a war. Let's get out of here."

The Pinkertons untied Rex Reed, helped him mount up, and tied him to a horse. Earl mounted his horse and took the lead as Brad tied Rex's feet under the horse's belly. Brad mounted his horse and they headed into the woods with the horses and their prisoner. When they reached the lookout post, they stopped and tied Bobby Cole to a horse, just the way they had done with Rex.

"A good raid," proclaimed Karl, squeezing the flanks of his horse. "It's time to put some distance between us and that gang."

CHAPTER 12

It was noon when they reached their campsite and dismounted. Brad and Earl tied Rex Reed and Bobby Cole to separate trees some distance away from Jade Wellman while Karl and Audrey guarded them.

"Would you like some lunch, Miss Benton?" asked Karl.

"Yes, I would. They didn't feed me much, and the food was terrible. Brad is a much better cook than those... those despicable men."

"Earl. Check your rifle and pistol, then set up the perimeter guard," directed Karl.

"I'm plenty hungry, too," said Earl. "But I can't be as hungry as Miss Benton. Those monsters should at least have had the decency to feed you."

"Audrey, I'll ask our friends some questions while you and your brother fix lunch," explained Karl. "Then I'll have some questions to ask you."

Brad made a small fire while Audrey started preparing their lunch. They watched Karl questioning the prisoners, and occasionally he would point toward Audrey. Brad told his sister about how closely he'd come to work with the Pinkertons and how they had found her. Then he thanked her for the button from her dress and the stripped leaves.

Brad arranged some rocks and set tin mugs and

plates on them. Audrey cut some bacon into small chunks and dropped them into a large frying pan.

"I'll do the rest of the cooking," said Brad. "Sit down and rest a bit, we've got the rest of the day and plenty to do."

When the bacon was done, Brad added two cans of beans. As soon as the beans started to bubble, Brad stood up and told his sister, "I'll let you announce lunch."

"Karl, Earl; beans, bacon, and tea," announced Audrey cheerily. "We have canned peaches for dessert."

As they ate lunch, Karl asked Audrey about the men at the ranch house. Earl took a plate of food and went back into the forest to serve as the camp lookout.

"Brad, thank you for bringing me some outlaw-catching clothes. My dress is dirty and torn; it was never meant to be worn while riding a horse."

"I guessed at your boot size, a little large was better than too small. And I thought you'd like some riding clothes."

"Much better for cooking over a campfire than a dress too," agreed his sister.

"Nice lunch, Audrey," said Karl. "Now that our strength has been rejuvenated with a wonderful meal of beans and bacon, and Audrey has donned her outlaw-catching clothes, are the two of you ready to pay another visit to the Rawlins Gang?"

"We do have a third of the gang," said Audrey thoughtfully. "I'm sure Sheriff Strong would like to see all of them behind bars."

"And they are horseless," added Brad. "They won't be expecting the Indians to return."

"Then now is the time to return," chuckled Karl. "I'm sure they haven't had lunch, so they'll be feeling hungry, angry, tired, and lonely. In general, they'll be rather unhappy."

"And three of the six are wounded," added Audrey. "Chite Hobbs is very badly wounded; I don't think he'll last the day."

Audrey told them about Chite's wound and praying that morning with Rex and Clete. Karl listened in silence as she recounted the morning. When she finished, Karl remained silent with his eyes closed for a moment, then stood, a look of determination on his face.

"Brad, you and I will get our horses ready, and tie six horses to a lead for the Rawlins Gang. Audrey, check the prisoners' gags. I don't want to give them the opportunity to talk to each other or holler for help."

There was a flurry of activity as the preparations for the return to the ranch house were finalized. Audrey checked the three men and then tied the horses to a lead rope as Brad and Karl brought them to her. When the horses were ready, the four of them mounted and headed back to meet the Rawlins Gang.

They walked the horses the last half mile, until Earl held up his hand. They stopped and dismounted. Earl checked the lookout site and returned, no one was on watch. The group continued on to a gully several hundred feet behind the barn and stopped. After the horses were picketed, Karl said, "Brad, Earl, scout out the barn. Audrey and I will be here waiting for you."

As Brad and Earl reached the brush a few feet behind the back of the barn, they could hear men inside arguing. Brad crept forward until he could look through a crack in the wall.

"All our horses, gone!" shouted Jake Rawlins. "Bobby Cole and Rex Reed are gone, too."

"No sign of the girl either," spat Curt Bender. "Her room was locked when we opened it, but she wasn't there. She just disappeared. It had to be Indians!"

"Indians could have stolen the horses," agreed Jake, somewhat calmer now. "I don't know about the girl. How could she get out of a locked room? And, if she did escape, where is she now? Or did the Indians take her? Let's go eat lunch and plan what we're going to do. It's a long walk back to Denver."

Brad and Earl quietly crept away from the barn, and then ran back to Audrey and Karl.

"I see," said Karl pondering Brad's report. "Brad, Earl, go ahead on foot. Audrey and I'll bring our four horses a little closer. We'll meet behind the barn."

Brad verified that the barn was empty before he and Earl entered. No sooner had they entered than they heard a man walking toward the barn, cursing. Earl motioned Brad to an empty stall close to the door. Earl scurried into a stall farther into the barn.

"What am I supposed to find in the barn that will help us?" grumbled Turk Atkins. "The horses are gone, the nurse is gone, two men are missing, Chite is dying, and Jake's partner has the money from the bank."

"Raise your hands and you'll get your questions

answered," said Earl, stepping out of his stall, his rifle pointed at Turk.

Turk stopped, trying to decide whether he should fight or surrender, when he heard a noise behind him.

"Slowly unbuckle your gunbelt and raise your hands, unless you want to join Chite," ordered Brad.

Turk meekly complied. After the gunbelt was removed, Turk put his hands behind his back so Brad could tie them. Earl's rifle barrel prodded Turk out the door and into the woods. Karl and Audrey had just arrived. Audrey promptly gagged Turk while Brad tied him to a tree.

"Earl," said Karl. "Take Audrey and go to the back of the house. Brad and I will wait until you're in place; then we'll ask Jake to surrender."

"He won't," countered Audrey. "He's a nasty, dishonest, despicable person. He lies to his own men. Don't trust him."

"I know you're right," said Karl. "But we have to try, or we'll be the same type of despicable person that he is."

"I'll look for your sign," said Brad, as Audrey and Earl entered the woods.

The .32 pistol hung heavy in Audrey's jacket pocket as she and Earl ran through the forest. "Brad said you're a good shot with that rifle," said Earl.

"Winchester makes an excellent rifle. This feels just like Brad's."

"It's the same model," said Earl. "We bought three of them yesterday, all just like the one you're carrying. Brad recommended it, and the gunsmith also said it was an excellent choice. And we have the benefit of one type of ammunition for all three rifles. Except for Karl, he's using the rifles we took from our prisoners."

A few minutes later Earl held up his hand and stopped. Turning to Audrey, he said softly, "This looks like a good place. We have some large trees, a few boulders, and a little gully."

"We also have a clear view of the rear and side of the house," said Audrey. "I'll wave to Brad."

Over at the barn, Brad said, "She just signaled that they're in place. Let's make their day a little more unpleasant."

From the safety of the barn, Karl shouted, "Jake Rawlins, this is Karl Braunsohn, Pinkerton Detective Agency. I've been deputized by Sheriff Strong to bring you in. It's all over. The Indians will be back. Surrender now or face the Indians tonight."

As soon as he finished shouting his message, Karl knelt behind the log wall of the barn. A moment later a bullet thudded into the side of the building.

Brad looked at Karl, "I don't think he wants to surrender. Let's go into the trees."

"I think you're right," conceded Brad as another bullet slammed into the barn. Taking aim at the front door of the ranch house, he continued, "But first, I'll disrupt their lunch." He squeezed his trigger and crawled into the forest with Brad.

From just inside the edge of the forest, Karl and Brad continued their fire. After each shot, they would crawl to another location, wait for the other to shoot, then wait a minute, carefully aim, and shoot again. The effect inside the house was pandemonium. There was no real lull in the gunfire and every shot came from a different location.

"Clete!" snarled Jake, kicking a chair in anger. "Go out the back door, into the woods, and work your way around to the barn. Get behind them. We can't stay like this until the Indians return tonight."

Clete carefully opened the back door, looked around, and stepped off the back porch. He took the privy path as he entered the woods. He had gone about twenty feet when he felt a rifle barrel poke him in the back.

"Now take your time. Lots of time," whispered Earl. "Unbuckle your gunbelt and let it drop to the ground. If you try anything, you should be aware that there's another rifle pointed at you."

"That's right," whispered Audrey. "My Ma hit Rex with a pistol at twice this distance, and I have a rifle. You should know that I'm a better shot than my Ma. I'm the true Annie Oakley of the family. I hope you make the right choice."

Clete dropped his rifle and gun belt and Earl tied him to a tree while Audrey quickly gagged him. Then they returned to the back of ranch house and waited. Only four men were left, including Chite who was near death.

"Rawlins," shouted Earl. "We've got Clete. It's over. Throw out your gun and come out."

To Audrey's surprise, Jake slowly opened the back door, threw out a pistol, and stepped out.

"You have my gun, now what?" shouted Jake, looking around.

Earl came out of the woods, a coil of rope in his hands. "Come down here, turn around, and put your hands behind your back," he commanded.

Jake stepped off the porch and turned around as ordered. However, when Earl started to tie his hands,

Jake struck, knocking him down. Earl rolled away and quickly stood up. He saw his pistol on the back porch and Jake rushing toward him at the same time. Guarding himself with his left arm, Earl punched Jake in the stomach with his right.

"You've got to do better than that, Pinky," sneered Jake, kicking at Earl.

The two men wrestled across the yard as Audrey watched, helpless, unable to shoot for fear of hitting Earl. She knew she had to wait. No matter what Jake did, she was going to assure the fight ended in Earl's favor, but she couldn't intervene yet. The fight moved onto the back porch. Then Jake hit Earl in the head, knocking him down. Earl shook his head; the ranch house and trees were spinning. Jake quickly scooped up the pistol he had thrown down earlier and turned toward Earl.

I've got to scare Jake, and do it with one shot, thought Audrey. Her rifle was already raised and aimed toward the house. With her finger on the trigger, she squeezed; her aim was just inches in front of Jake's face. The bullet struck the center of a washtub hanging on the side of the ranch house.

The tub rang like a bad church bell. Momentarily stunned by the rifle shot, the whine of the bullet, and the ringing of the tub, Jake felt like he was inside a belfry; his mouth opened, and he looked into the forest, searching for the source of the rifle shot.

"That is your only warning!" shouted Audrey. "Toss your pistol toward me now."

Jake tossed the pistol as ordered.

"Good! Now drop your pants around your ankles and

face the house." Jake hesitated, so Audrey shouted, "NOW!"

"My pants! Did you say my pants?" he shrieked, not believing what he had heard.

"Your pants, and quickly," ordered Audrey. "I don't like you; I don't like your kind; I don't like what your gang members did to me, my brother, and my mother. If your pants aren't down by the time I count to three, my rifle will do it for you, with you in them."

"ONE!"

"TWO!"

Jake quickly unbuckled his pants, dropping them around his ankles, and faced the house.

"Brad! Karl!" shouted Audrey. "I've got Jake. I need your help now. I don't know where Curt and Clay are."

"Stay where you are!" shouted Karl. "Don't take any chances. If he tries something, starts talking to you, or even moves, shoot."

Lowering his voice, Karl said, "Brad, go to the right and I'll go left. Stay in the woods. I'll meet you in back of the house."

Brad ran through the trees with his rifle. His sister hadn't said anything about Earl; she obviously didn't want to let the men in the house know what had happened. Unfortunately, that meant Brad and Karl didn't know either.

As the back of the ranch house came into view, Brad saw a man, his hands raised, and his pants around his ankles. Earl was trying to get up, but he was still on his hands and knees.

"Rawlins!" shouted Brad. "Start backing up now; and do it slowly. Keep your hands in the air."

Jake Rawlins did as Brad ordered. He hopped and

109

stumbled down the porch steps with his pants around his ankles. By the time he reached the woods and was backing down the path to the privy, Karl had arrived.

"Stop!" commanded Karl. "Now a gentleman really shouldn't be in front of a lady with his pants on the ground. Pull them up, then put your hands behind you."

Again, Jake did as ordered. As soon as he placed his hands behind him, Audrey stepped out of the bushes.

Anger flashing in her eyes, she poked her rifle barrel into his stomach. Jake looked down but did nothing.

"You vile piece of garbage," she hissed. Motioning to Karl and Earl, she continued, "These two men are part of the reason you're not in the same condition as Chite Hobbs. I could have shot you a few minutes ago. Any judge, any jury, any lawman would have congratulated me. But Reverend Wesley told me that I should not take the life of another human being, except in self-defense. The right to take the life of a human must remain with the government and with the Lord. You have Reverend Wesley to thank that you're still alive."

Jake glared at Audrey, then spat on her, and sneered as the blob of spittle darkening her shirt. Audrey looked at her shirt, then at the sneering man. In one swift movement, she drew back her rifle, turned the weapon around, slamming the rifle butt hard into Rawlins' stomach, knocking the wind out of him. He lay on the ground gasping for air, as Brad tied his hands and gagged him. Together, Brad and Karl pulled him to a tree and bound him to it.

"Clay, you're next!" shouted Karl. "Do the same thing your boss did, but not too fast."

Clay slowly came out the back door, dropped his
110

rifle, and turned to face the house. Then, as Jake had done, he started walking backwards slowly into the forest.

"Now put your hands behind your back," ordered Karl.

Clay slowly placed his hands behind his back. Brad tied his hands then tied him to another tree, gagged.

"Now, what do we do about Curt?" said Brad.

"I'll call to him," said Audrey.

"Curt!" shouted Audrey. "Curt Bender. Jake is captured. All of your partners are captured. Come out and give yourself up."

Audrey's plea was met with silence. She repeated her demand.

"Audrey," said a weak voice. "It's Chite; Curt's down. You can come in, but be careful."

Circling the house, Karl entered through the front door at the same time Earl entered through the back door. "He's in here on the floor," said Earl, kicking a six-shooter away from the man sprawled on the floor.

Karl checked Chite, and then joined Earl in the kitchen. "Check him out," said Karl.

Earl rolled Curt over onto his back, but no response. Then he saw a big red lump on his forehead, and a large cast iron skillet on the floor. "I think this skillet got him," said Earl feeling Curt's neck. "He has a strong pulse, and there's no bleeding."

Audrey looked at the skillet, picked up a flat piece of shiny metal from the floor, and said, "It was the skillet. I probably knocked it off the wall when I fired the warning shot at Jake Rawlins. This looks like a flattened rifle slug."

"Audrey," said Chite hoarsely.

111

"Yes, Chite," replied Audrey, instinctively going over and holding his hand.

"Thank you for praying with me this morning. I can't see too well any more, so I know I'm about gone. Please say a prayer for me when you bury me."

"I will," promised Audrey, tears streaking down her face. "I'll say a prayer for you."

Audrey held Chite's massive hand, which dwarfed her small fingers. Chite talked softly, and Audrey leaned close to hear him. When he finished speaking, he gave Audrey's hand a gentle squeeze. Slowly Chite's grip loosened, and his labored breathing stopped. Audrey continued holding his limp hand for some time. She said a silent prayer for the man that she had helped in his final hours. This was the man who had arranged for two other outlaws to help her escape from abandonment and certain death in the rugged mountains. Now Audrey prayed for the Lord to forgive him for his past, and to accept his prayer asking for forgiveness that she had guided him through earlier that day. Now his eternal fate rested in the hands of the Eternal Father.

After Curt Bender regained consciousness and recovered from his tussle with the frying pan, he and Turk Atkins dug a grave and lowered Chite's blanket-wrapped body into the earth. Audrey said a prayer, and then Curt, Rex, and Turk filled the grave. Turk placed a number of large rocks on top of the grave to help prevent wild animals from unearthing Chite's remains. Karl and Earl stood back from the grave; their rifles cradled in their arms. Jake remained gagged and tied to a tree.

Nothing was said as Curt, Rex, and Turk, one at a time, mounted their horses. After they were mounted, Earl and Brad tied their hands to the saddle horn and then their feet to a rope under the belly of the horse. Earl tied each outlaw's horse to the next outlaw's horse. When the gang members' five horses were tied into one line, at Karl's signal, they left single file for the camp where the other three gang members were waiting. Chite's riderless horse, tied to a lead behind Audrey, was the last to leave the ranch house.

CHAPTER 13

Friday afternoon, 10 June 1881: Brad, Audrey, the Pinkertons, and the last six members of the Rawlins gang arrived at the camp. The Pinkertons helped the prisoners off their horses, and Karl proceeded to question them.

Karl talked to Jake Rawlins last. "Well, Mr. Rawlins; it seems that your partner, Cornelius Calhoun, has absconded with the money and left you with nothing." Rawlins looked up angrily but said nothing. "You do know that Mr. Calhoun is your partner, or did you just give him the money?"

Brad pulled Karl aside and said just loudly enough to e overheard, "Please don't tell him that Calhoun led us to him."

Jake looked up and shouted, "That skunk led you to me! I'll take care of him, jail or no jail."

"That won't be necessary, Mr. Rawlins," stated Audrey. "That skunk has already proven his ability to fail. We'll capture him shortly; then he'll join you in jail."

Earl and Brad untied Bobby Cole and Jade Wellman from their trees, removed their gags, and gave them some water.

"Thank you," said Jade. "I promise not to talk if you just won't gag me."

"I'll consider that," replied Earl. "But the decision is Detective Braunsohn's, not mine."

The prisoners were readied for their trip, and Karl had them assembled around the burned-out campfire. "Several of you have asked not to be gagged. If you don't talk, I won't gag you. Understood?"

"I'll talk if I want to," spat Jake loudly. "I may be tied, but I can still talk to my men."

"I understand what you want," affirmed Karl. "But I also understand what we want. I'll gag you. Earl?"

Earl placed a gag in Rawlins' mouth, but not before Jake had cursed and threatened everyone within earshot. Karl and Audrey kept their rifles ready as Earl and Brad helped the men onto their horses. Each had their hands tied to the saddle horns, and their feet tied together under the horse.

When Rex Reed's time came, he turned to Audrey and said, "Miss Audrey. Please accept my apology for the terrible language Jake used a few minutes ago. You did nothing to deserve exposure to such language."

"Thank you, Rex."

Clete started to put his hands on the saddle horn to mount his horse, but stopped and said, "Miss Benton. Thank you for treating our wounds, and for helping Chite today. I'm sorry you were kidnapped. While you were in your room, the men talked about you. We didn't understand why you were kidnapped."

"Chite told me, just before he died," explained Audrey. "He heard Cornelius Calhoun and Jake talking last night. Jake suspected that I had recognized him

115

as the gang leader. So he and Calhoun ordered my kidnapping. Jake was not going to free me after your wounds healed. He was going to abandon me in the woods and let me fend for myself."

"Brad, Earl, Audrey - it's time to head out. Take your places," directed Karl.

Brad, Audrey, and the Pinkertons mounted their horses. Karl addressed the prisoners: "You all asked not to be gagged, except for Mr. Rawlins. That's fine with me. However, remember that there will be absolutely no talking. Is that understood?"

There was a chorus of yeses and nods of agreement from the prisoners.

"Brad, roll 'em out," ordered Karl in a strong voice.

Brad led the column of horses out of the camp. Audrey and Earl were in the center, and Karl brought up the rear. Sometime later they passed the rock slide. Brad stopped where the buggy horse had been tethered earlier in the week. Karl and Earl tied the prisoners to trees while Brad and Audrey made a campfire and started an evening meal of beans and bacon for everyone.

"I'll go into town and see Sheriff Strong while Earl stays with you and the prisoners," said Karl. "I don't want to parade this group down the main street and spook Mr. Calhoun. Earl, keep a good lookout until I return with the sheriff. Brad, Audrey; I need you to help Earl. I also want you to stay out of sight in the event that Calhoun comes looking for the Rawlins Gang before I return with the sheriff."

"We'll melt into the woods as soon as we clean up the dishes," replied Brad.

116

"I'm going to spread the word that we failed to find you," said Karl. "I will, however, get word to your mother that both of you are safe, but to act as if Audrey's still missing."

Karl rode up to the sheriff's office, dismounted, and slowly stepped onto the boardwalk. He stopped, looking up and down the boardwalk; and took note of a man watching him from the saloon across the street. He entered the sheriff's office.

"Good afternoon," said Karl, grasping Sheriff Strong's hand while slipping a note into it. "I'm sorry to report that we found no trace of the girl. If you wish, I can stop by tomorrow and give you a full report."

"I'm sorry, too," said the sheriff, catching the note. "I was hoping that you'd find her. I'm in court in the morning; maybe you can stop by tomorrow afternoon and fill me in on what you did find."

"That's fine with me," said Karl. "Tomorrow afternoon."

Karl left the sheriff's office, mounted his horse, and rode away at a fast walk. He took no apparent notice of the man leaning against the side of the sheriff's office, next to the open window.

About ten minutes later, Sheriff Strong told his deputy he was going for an early supper. And then to check on Dan Black and the prisoners at the hospital.

Wong's Cafe was getting ready for the evening customers when the back door opened and Karl Braunsohn entered. He nodded at Sae-Jin and said,

"I'd like to eat in your kitchen tonight, I'm expecting a friend shortly for a private meeting."

"Use my father's office, Mr. Braunsohn," she said. "It will be very private for your discussion about Audrey Benton."

"How do you know what the meeting is about?" asked a surprised Karl.

"Everyone in town knows you and her brother went searching for her. I'm sure that Brad was very helpful. Excuse me now, I'll send Sheriff Strong back when he arrives."

Sae-Jin quietly left, allowing Karl to ponder how she knew so much. Before long Sheriff Strong entered the back door of the cafe and took a seat in the small, cramped office with Karl.

"What do you have?"

Karl gave the sheriff a quick summary of events and then a request. Sheriff Strong gave a low whistle.

Karl continued, "I need a large wagon and tarp to take the west road after dark. We can load the prisoners in the wagon, cover it with a tarp, and, hopefully, take it to the fort. I'm sure the commander will keep the prisoners for you. We have to keep the capture of the gang a secret until we have Cornelius Calhoun in jail."

"I agree," said the sheriff. "The commanding officer of the fort has worked with me in the past. I'm sure he'll do so again, especially when I explain the circumstances to him."

"I'll return to the campsite and tell them to expect you with a large wagon sometime after dark tonight."

Karl rode into the campsite just before sunset, singing "Streets of Laredo," the agreed-upon password, or, in this case, pass-song. A small campfire was burning, and Earl's bedroll was next to his saddle. Brad and Audrey had set up their bedrolls in a more secluded spot, just in case Cornelius Calhoun made an unexpected appearance.

"Well, what were you able to arrange?" asked Earl.

"The sheriff will arrive later tonight with a wagon. And my appearance at the sheriff's office was duly noted. When I left, there was a man leaning against the front of building who heard through the window what I told the sheriff."

"Did you actually tell the sheriff that we had the gang?"

"Not at his office, but we met privately at Wong's Café – in Wong's office. It was cramped, but the food was good as usual."

"Anything else of interest?" asked Earl.

"Yes. The town knows we are searching for Audrey. Wong's daughter told me that our search is a topic of discussion among their patrons. I'm glad I used a note to set up the meeting with the sheriff."

"Then tomorrow we'll start tracking Mr. Cornelius Calhoun," concluded Earl.

It was quite late by the time all of the prisoners had been loaded into the sheriff's wagon and covered with a tarp. The prisoners agreed to say nothing until the sheriff told them they could, except for Jake Rawlins, who remained gagged.

Brad and Karl Braunsohn took the lead and Audrey and Earl took the rear with the sheriff's wagon in the middle. The prisoners' horses were tied to the rear of the wagon.

"How far to the fort?" asked Brad.

"About an hour," said Karl. "We should arrive around midnight. The commander is expecting us."

"I still don't understand how Cornelius Calhoun got tied in with the Rawlins Gang," wondered Brad. "He appears to be a successful businessman."

"Yes, he certainly has that appearance," agreed Karl. However, can you tell me what his business is? Does he have a wife and children? Does he have a home? When these and other questions are answered, we'll know why he partnered up with Jake Rawlins."

An hour later the outline of the fort could be seen in the moonlight. When they reached the gate, Karl stopped. Sheriff Strong told the guard who they were and that the commander was expecting them.

"He said you'd be here around midnight, Sheriff. I'll have the gate opened and get the commander."

Two soldiers took the prisoners from the wagon and led them into a room with a heavy door.

"Hands out," ordered Brad as each man reached the door of their common cell. He untied their hands, and they entered the room rubbing their wrists and then their back sides.

"That wagon ride was a mite hard on your south end, isn't it?" granted Earl.

"Sure is," agreed Rex Reed, rubbing his buttocks. "I never thought I'd look forward to a jail cell, or should I say stockade since this is an army jail?"

120

When the last prisoner was untied, the soldiers closed and locked the door.

"Next we go to the commander's office," said Earl as they left the stockade, the guard's lantern lighting the way. "Let's see what your sister and the sheriff have been doing."

"Well, Sheriff, the gang is well secured," said the commander as Brad and Earl entered his office. "Let's go to the infirmary and check on the wounded."

Sheriff Strong stood in the doorway and listened to the doctor. "Good medical work, Audrey. You removed the bullet and the small piece of Clete's shirt. If you hadn't removed the piece of cloth, the wound would have festered and, well, Clete would probably be in the hills with his partner, Chite."

"Thank you," said Audrey, blushing. "I did what Pa and Doc Adams taught me. I'm glad they taught me what to do."

"I never thought you'd actually treat so many wounds," remarked Brad. "I know you helped Sarah Davis deliver a baby, but you didn't do it alone. And we helped Pa after Duke Badger shot him, but that was just fixing him up so we could get him to Doc Adams."

His sister nodded in agreement, "I know."

"Audrey," said the doctor, "You can be a good doctor, or nurse, if you want to. You have a natural talent for medicine. It's the Lord's gift to you; use it wisely."

Brad, Audrey, and the two Pinkertons watched Sheriff Strong's wagon until the darkness enveloped it. "Let's get back to our camp," said Karl. It must be one in the morning, and we have a lot of things to do tomorrow."

"I'm tired," said Audrey. "But I'm not sleepy."

"You'll probably learn about that at medical school," said Karl. "I don't know how to explain it, but I feel the same way, and I believe Brad and Earl do, too."

"I know I do," said Brad.

Sometime later as they left the road to their campsite, Brad said, "How about a cup of hot tea, Audrey?"

"I'd really like that, especially if you hand me the mug while you have a towel draped across your arm and speak like an English butler."

They dismounted in the moonlight. While Brad and Earl took care of the horses, Audrey built a small fire. Karl positioned the saddles and bedrolls around the fire, then helped Audrey. The pot of water for tea was on the fire by the time everyone's chores were finished. The bedrolls were opened in front of the saddles and readied for the night. Tired bodies hunched around the fire as the tea water started to boil.

Audrey put a pinch of tea in the water and announced, "The tea will be ready in a few minutes."

"Here's the last of the oatmeal cookies," said Karl, passing a waxed-paper bag to Brad.

The four of them sat around the fire, eating the cookies, talking about the day's events, and discussing what they were going to do come daylight.

Detective Braunsohn commented, "I'm sure there is a reward for some or all of the gang."

"It can help pay for your medical training," said Brad.

122

"True, but I need to find a medical school that accepts women."

"I'm sure one exists," said Detective Martin, "I saw a woman doctor in Chicago last year."

"I'm tired, this has been a very long day," said Brad. "Audrey, what about you?"

"Now I'm sleepy," she said shaking her cup dry. "I hope I stay awake long enough to cover myself with a blanket before I fall asleep."

CHAPTER 14

Saturday morning, 11 June 1881: Karl Braunsohn spoke in a hushed voice to the hotel manager. The manager nodded in agreement. "I understand. I'll tell her as soon as she comes down. You can wait in my office, Mr. Braunsohn."

He had barely entered the manager's office when he heard the manager say, "Mrs. Benton, I have a message for you."

"Yes, Mr. Girard, what is it?"

"Mr. Braunsohn is in my office. He'd like to speak to you privately," he said motioning to the office door.

Abby entered, and a man in the lobby saw Karl's somber face. Once the door was closed, he held his finger over his lips and whispered, "We're being watched, so listen carefully. Your daughter is safe. We rescued her yesterday; in fact, she saved my partner's life."

Abby looked at Karl, a wave of relief swept over her. Then she cocked her head sideways and whispered in return, "I don't understand the need for secrecy."

"We need to catch the ringleader. And to do that, we need him to believe that we haven't found your daughter. If anyone asks you, I've told you that we're still looking; and that your son left us to search alone for his sister. Tell no one that we found your daughter."

"Where are my children?" asked Abby, tears streaking down her face.

"They're at a campsite about an hour west of town. The only ones that know are you, me, Detective Martin, and Sheriff Strong."

"Thank you for finding my daughter," sobbed Abby, impulsively giving Karl a hug.

Karl, holding her by the shoulders, looked into her eyes, and continued, "We hope to capture the ringleader by the end of the day. Now I'm going to leave and close the door. Take your time and look concerned when you come out. Go have breakfast, and if anyone asks, we're still searching for your daughter. And please, don't look so relieved. Look worried, look concerned, and don't wipe your tears away."

Karl left the manager's office and closed the door. "Give her a few minutes to compose herself," he told the manager. "And can you arrange for her to have a private, secluded table for breakfast? We're still searching for her daughter."

"I'll assure that she has a private table," confirmed Mr. Girard.

Karl's next stop was Skeets' livery. "Skeets," he greeted. "Those were good horses, but I'll need them for a few more days. We're still searching for the girl."

"I understand," said Skeets nodding. "Law work is never fast."

"If you see Mr. Calhoun again, please send word to Sheriff Strong immediately. Send a boy with a message that says his new saddle is in. He'll know what it means."

"Sure, Mr. Braunsohn," replied Skeets. "You can keep those horses a few more days, all week if you like."

Karl stopped in at the General Store, the Silver Platter, Wong's Cafe, and Delmonico's Restaurant, leaving similar instructions. Then he met Earl at the hotel.

"Let's go to the banks together," he said. "I'll ask the questions, while you keep your eyes open."

After visiting several banks, Earl remarked, "Mr. Calhoun appears to be in need of money."

"That could explain his partnership with Jake Rawlins," said Karl. "They didn't get that much money in the robbery, and he apparently still needs more, quite a bit more."

"Same story from all the banks. He's got a good gold mine, and just needs cash to start it up," said Earl. "However, the bankers have heard that same story from thousands of men."

"Let's stop in and see some of our lawyer friends," suggested Karl. "We may find a few more pieces to this puzzle."

"I'm sorry, Mr. Braunsohn," said the lawyer, gently sliding a document to the side of his desk so that Earl could read it. "As a lawyer, all discussions with my client are private. I cannot, nor will I, discuss them with you, the sheriff, or any other representative of the law. However, I also feel compelled to express my shock that any man would kidnap a young girl. Further, it is an outrage that after using her nursing services, he would order her abandoned in the mountains to fend for herself, which would mean almost certain death."

"I understand your position," acknowledged Karl as

they stood up to leave. "You cannot violate your oath of confidentiality with a client."

Outside, Earl suggested, "We should check with the sheriff, he may have learned something."

"I think you're right," agreed Karl, stopping to write a note on a piece of paper.

"You'll need someone to deliver that note," said Earl. "I think I see our messenger now."

"Excuse me, Sister," said Karl, taking off his hat. "Would you accept a donation to The Sisters of Charity?"

"Most certainly," replied the nun. "May I ask your name?"

"Here's my card," said Karl, handing her his Pinkerton card and showing her his badge. "And would you be so kind as to deliver this note to Sheriff Strong?"

Karl handed the sister a folded sheet of paper, and a twenty-dollar gold piece. The nun accepted the note and the money, and placed them in her pocket, but looked at him questioningly.

Karl explained, "This is about the young lady and her brother who saved the lives of Deputy Black and two of the bank robbers on Tuesday. I need a trusted messenger to personally hand this note to the sheriff. No one must know what I've just said. That is why I'm asking you."

"Hail Mary, by the grace of God. I will also pray for your success at our afternoon vespers."

The two Pinkertons watched the nun continue down the street. Karl nodded at a passing trolley and said, "I'm ready for an early lunch at Wong's. His kitchen is usually rather quiet on Saturdays."

Several minutes later they got off the streetcar and walked to Wong's Cafe.

"You are early," said Sae-Jin. "But you came for a private meeting, am I correct?

"Correct, as usual," replied Karl. "May we eat in your kitchen?"

"Certainly, how many more will be coming?"

"Just the sheriff," said Karl, as they went into the kitchen.

Earl was starting his second cup of coffee when the sheriff entered the kitchen from the alley. "I'm starting to act like a Pinkerton," muttered the sheriff. "I told my men that Deputy Black needed to see me at the hospital, then I was coming here for an early lunch. So, I hopped a streetcar to the hospital, which, I'm sure, was duly reported by the man in front of my office. But, pray tell, how did you get a nun to deliver the note?"

"I needed someone I could trust, and suddenly, there was a nun walking toward me," said Karl. "So I asked her if she would deliver a message for me. I also explained why I wanted her, not someone else, to deliver the message."

"Divine intervention," professed Earl with a smile.

"What do you have?" asked the sheriff as he ran his fingers through his hair. "I've come up dry; nothing."

Karl related what they had discovered, and the sheriff let out a low whistle. "So," he said, "Cornelius Calhoun got Jake Rawlins to help finance the startup of his gold mine. That explains the robbery, Calhoun following Audrey, and her kidnapping."

"He also has several loans coming due from his bank," added Earl. "He is a man in dire financial straits. He

128

is desperate for money. Without it, he'll lose his mine, his horse, his stock in the new Denver & New Orleans Railroad - everything he owns - to the bank. His lawyer insisted on maintaining his client's confidentiality. Yet he did, entirely by accident, position a document on his desk so that I could read it."

"Calhoun made a large payment on his loan, which bought him another month," said Karl. "But he still needs more money."

"We have more than enough evidence to arrest him," said the sheriff. "And it's vital that we find him before he discovers that we're looking for him. I don't want to spook him and have him disappear. I've already put out the word to a number of trusted businessmen. It is just a matter of time."

"I'll take some newspapers and food out to our young Pinkertons," said Earl. "They might be out there several more days. I'll stay with them tonight."

"Be sure to tell them that I told their mother that they're both safe," requested Karl.

Brad and Audrey sat on a small knoll overlooking their campsite. "Thank you for letting me take a nap this morning," said Audrey. "I don't know when I've ever been so tired before."

"You can be on watch while I take a nap this afternoon."

"And thanks again for bringing me a set of outlaw-catching clothes. It's not nice riding in that kind of dress. My legs are still tender from rubbing against the saddle, my bottom has a blister on it from the cheap saddle they tied me to, and my feet hurt because my shoes weren't meant for riding."

"But other than that, everything is fine," said Brad, trying to hide a subtle smirk.

His sister studied her brother's face a moment, then gave him a knowing smile. "I guess I shouldn't be complaining; I have so much to be thankful for."

"Are you ready to talk about your kidnapping?"

"I think so."

She told him about the buggy ride, then being led on horseback. "I stripped some branches, just in case you found my trail. Your wolf howl really gave me hope. I knew you had found me. The next morning when I examined Chite again, he told me that Calhoun was not going to let me go, that my life was in danger. He said I could trust Clete and Rex to help me escape if the opportunity arose."

"Did Chite know he was going to die?" asked Brad.

"He asked me, and I told him the truth. He asked me to pray for him. Rex and Clete protected me from Jake while I helped Chite ask the Lord to forgive his sins."

Audrey looked out into the forest, her mind somewhere else. Finally, Brad said, "I hear a horse coming, and its rider is singing. It must be Earl."

Earl dismounted at the campsite, removed his saddlebags, and looked around. He saw Brad and Audrey coming down from the knoll toward him.

"I brought some newspapers, bacon, beans, cookies, canned peaches, makings for pancakes, eggs, syrup, and I don't remember what else."

"We're ready for lunch," said Brad. "I'll start the fire. What did you find out?"

"Just enough to confirm your suspicions," replied Earl. "Calhoun is in debt. He's about to lose his mine, so he let Jake Rawlins buy a 50% stake for $7,000. That's a little less than what was taken from the bank."

They continued talking as the bacon was placed in the frying pan. Brad and Earl assembled some rocks and branches and made a table of sorts.

"Bacon and eggs," sighed Brad. "After all those beans, this is a real feast."

Brad poured three mugs of tea while Audrey placed thick strips of bacon and fried eggs onto the plates Earl had laid on the makeshift table.

"Earl," asked Audrey nodding at him. "Will you please bless our meal?"

Earl said a short grace and they began eating.

"Did you tell our mother that we found Audrey?" asked Brad.

"Yes, Karl told her this morning. However, she is supposed to act as if we're still searching for you."

"More bacon?" asked Audrey, as she took the skillet off of the fire.

"Yes, please," replied Brad, holding out his plate.

"What about Calhoun?" asked Audrey. "Have you found him?"

"No, and that has us worried," answered Earl. "After lunch, you two make yourselves scarce until I return this evening. Karl, Sheriff Strong, and I are being watched. Everything that can be overheard, where we go, who we talk to, is being reported back to someone. We believe that someone is Cornelius Calhoun."

"Did you know that Rawlins and Calhoun were going to abandon Audrey in the mountains?" asked Brad.

"Rex Reed and Clete Corbin told Karl that. They both said they may rob and steal, but that they couldn't take part in hurting a young lady, particularly Audrey. What did you do to create such loyalty from them?" asked Earl.

"I cared for them. I helped Chite in his last hours, and I prayed for him," said Audrey, a tear streaking down her cheek. "Rex and Clete sheltered me from Jake while I did it. Chite also told me that I could trust Rex and Clete to help me escape."

They talked more about Audrey's time in captivity and shared theories about Cornelius Calhoun. When they had finished eating, Earl helped clean up.

"Thanks for the lunch," said Earl. "I've got to go back and help Karl track down Calhoun. You two be careful. He probably knows we're looking for him, and he may come this way to check on his mine."

CHAPTER 15

Noon, Saturday, 11 June 1881: As soon as Earl rode away, Brad and Audrey returned to the knoll above their campsite.

"What would you be doing, or thinking, if you were Calhoun?" asked Audrey.

Brad pondered the question for a minute. "I'd be concerned that Jade Wellman never showed up in town. You also said that there wasn't much food at the house, so I'd want to find out why one of Rawlins' men hadn't come into town for more supplies. I'd have the feeling that something wasn't right, and I'd want to investigate."

"I believe he'd take the back route to the ranch house, and then follow the road with the rock slide back to town," said Audrey.

"We should get ready," cautioned Brad. "We may be welcoming Mr. Calhoun to our campsite later today."

Brad and Audrey moved their shelter on the knoll behind some bushes. The move of a few feet was enough so that it couldn't be seen from the campsite. From their shelter, however, they could see the campsite and the abandoned road leading to it.

"You need a holster for Ma's .32 pistol," said Brad.

"How about a sort of sling you can wear over your shirt? It would be covered by your jacket."

"We can use my dress and petticoat. They're torn and dirty. I'll have to buy new ones when we get back to town."

Brad cut the dress into strips with his knife and worked with Audrey to create a makeshift shoulder holster. Ten minutes later, Audrey put on her jacket over the new holster, nodded, and said, "It works." She gently removed the pistol, and then reinserted it. "It's not easy to put in, but it is easy to take out. Success!"

"Now for the bedrolls," said Brad. "We need to make the campsite look lived in. But first, let's look and listen."

They were quiet for a minute. Audrey broke the silence, "All I hear is birds and the chatter of squirrels."

"Good," said Brad. "Let's work on the camp."

Together, they created some holes in the paths leading to the camp. They hid the holes with branches and leaves. Their saddles and bedrolls were moved just far enough into the bushes to force someone to come close to see if they were occupied.

"No food for me," said Earl. "I had an early lunch with our two young Pinkertons. But I will have a cup of coffee."

"I've gotten the word out to about twenty businessmen to let me know if they see Calhoun," reported the sheriff.

"I've left the word with about fifteen businessmen as well," added Karl. "If they see Calhoun, they'll send word to you."

The sheriff continued. "A bartender reported that a gambler was asking about Jade Wellman. The gambler alleged that Jade owes him some money and was supposed to make a payment Thursday. However, the bartender said that Jade Wellman has never gambled."

"It sounds like Calhoun is looking for Jade," reasoned Earl.

"If I were Calhoun, I'd be getting concerned," said Karl.

"Why?" asked Earl. "Jake gave him the money to postpone foreclosure on his mine, stock, house, and horse for a month."

"You do have a point there," conceded the sheriff. "By the way, how are Brad and Audrey?"

"Fine. I told them that I would be out this evening for dinner and would spend the night with them."

The three lawmen discussed Calhoun and the kidnapping while they had a piece of Wong's apple pie and another cup of coffee.

"Well, I should go back to the office," said the sheriff as he stood up. "I've got good men, but not enough. If we don't find Calhoun by tomorrow, maybe we should bring in Brad and Audrey. What are your thoughts?"

"I agree," said Karl. "I'm beginning to think that Calhoun knows something has gone wrong and has skipped town. He has nothing to stay for other than the mine, which he's probably going to lose anyway."

"I agree. If I were in his shoes, I'd be on my way to San Francisco by now," said Earl. "It's not worth the risk for him to remain in Denver."

"Sheriff," said Deputy Jim Murray, standing in the doorway to Wong's office. "A boy delivered this note for you a few minutes ago. The boy said it was personal and important, for your eyes only."

Sheriff Strong opened the envelope, read the message, and then looked around at the. Reading aloud, he said, "Your man suspects something is wrong. He's going after the girl and her brother. It's signed, 'Joe, Delmonico's Restaurant.'"

CHAPTER 16

Saturday Afternoon, 11 June 1881: Cornelius Calhoun walked back and forth in an abandoned miner's cabin outside Denver. He stared at the ashes in the fireplace and thought; *Jade Wellman should have been here by now. He didn't arrive Thursday as he was supposed to, or Friday, either. Now it's Saturday, and still no word from Jake Rawlins. They're still hunting for the girl and the Rawlins Gang.*

He stormed out of the cabin and started to mount his horse, then looked at his horse's hoofprint in the dirt. "A groove!" he shouted. Quickly, he checked his horse's rear shoe. He saw the groove that Brad had filed in the horseshoe and suddenly felt nauseous, as if a horse had kicked him in the stomach.

"It had to be that Benton kid that did that. I don't know how he found my horse. I didn't think he was that smart. Well, I'll show that kid what smart is. I'm going to backtrack and get him. But first, I'm going to the ranch house to get his sister."

Angry, he yanked the reins around and cruelly jabbed his spurs into the horse. The horse screamed in pain as it galloped away. Bleeding from the jabbed spurs, it galloped all the way to the gang's empty ranch house.

U

"We've got to get to Brad and Audrey before Calhoun does," declared the sheriff. "We need to go now. We can't leave them alone."

"Wait," cautioned Karl. "He knows that we're looking for him, and he suspects that that something has gone wrong. But he doesn't know where they're hiding. It's possible he could follow us and then bushwhack us all."

"The man did arrange Audrey's kidnapping," said Earl. "I wouldn't put any action past him. We need to go separately for our sake as well as theirs."

They discussed several possible courses of action, finally deciding upon a plan. "I'll ride out alone and hide off of the road about ten minutes this side of their campsite," said Karl. "The sheriff will ride out about ten minutes later and go alone to the campsite. Earl, you follow the sheriff, but continue past the campsite. Then circle back."

"Karl, give a whistle when I ride past you," said the sheriff. That way I'll know you're okay. If I don't hear a whistle, at least I'll know something has gone wrong."

"Do the same for me," said Earl. "And I'll whistle when I approach the campsite, too."

U

The changes to the campsite were significant, but not easily seen. The two Bentons continued their preparations for a possible visit from Calhoun. Brad took his coil of rope, cut off a length, and bent a sapling

138

down. After tying down the top of the young tree, he carefully loaded it with thorny vines.

"I'll wrap the rope with a small piece of my white petticoat," said Audrey.

"We've got a few more saplings to load," said Brad. "I don't know how much time we have, but I think we're about out. We have to hurry."

"We're done," said Audrey with satisfaction as they loaded another tree. "The last tree has been loaded and flagged."

"Careful," warned Brad. "We have a four-legged friend living under that old tree."

"Thanks, I don't want to disturb our friend."

"Our dear four-legged friend," said Brad.

"Brad Benton, I've seen that look before. You wouldn't."

"Yes, I would, wouldn't you?"

"Well," said Audrey, a sly smile on her face. "I think we should. Let's call it operation welcome.

They worked feverishly, completing one last trap for Cornelius Calhoun. When they finished, Brad was panting for air. "I need to rest," he said. "But we should hide now."

The two of them ran to their shelter and laid down to catch their breath.

"Gone!" shouted Calhoun to the empty house. "Everyone's gone. The horses, the Rawlins Gang, even the girl. That Benton kid did this, I know it."

Calhoun let his anger subside; then started looking at the barn and house with close attention to detail.

With his anger in check, he finally saw the bullet holes in the house and the barn.

There's been a shootout, he thought. *There are rifle and pistol shell casings on the floor and bullet holes in the walls. But what happened to Rawlins and his men? They haven't been in Denver. The gambler and his men have been watching the sheriff and the hotel; they've heard nothing. The girl's mother is still crying about her daughter's kidnapping. The sheriff says he's heard nothing and has no leads. It doesn't make sense. Rawlins is a partner in my gold mine; he said he was going to get rich with me. I'll go back to town, take the abandoned road. Maybe I'll see something.*

Brad and Audrey had recovered from their work, were breathing normally and talking in whispers. "All that work may have been in vain," sighed Audrey.

"Possibly," said Brad. "But it's like putting buckets of sand and water in our house when the arsonist was in Riverton. It was a waste of effort until he set fire to our house."

"True," she conceded. "And the day isn't over yet."

They lay in their shelter, listening and watching; listening for a horse or a voice; looking for a man on horseback or on foot. But there was nothing.

"Audrey," whispered Brad. "Do you hear that?"

She listened intently, then said, "I don't hear anything."

"I know, not even the birds," whispered Brad. "Something, or someone, is coming."

"Look to the west."

140

Brad looked and saw a few birds fly out of the trees. Then a deer ran past their camp, splashing through the nearby stream.

"Let him come to us," advised Brad. "We're not in a rush."

"Right," said his sister. "Let him get to our dummies sleeping against the saddles in the lean-to. Then, it'll be time to act."

Cornelius Calhoun dismounted and slowly approached the campsite, honing in on the gently curling smoke of the campfire. Pistol drawn, he quietly approached the two figures reclining against the saddles. At distance of about 10 feet, he stopped and raised his pistol.

"Now," whispered Brad.

Audrey had already aimed, so she gently squeezed the trigger, which dropped a large dead tree branch on the burrow of the four-legged friend in the dead tree.

Calhoun yelped and ducked behind a tree.

"Now," whispered Audrey.

Brad squeezed his trigger, and a bullet whacked into a tree branch, ripping it away from the trunk as it fell onto Calhoun's head. He immediately crawled backwards, to hide behind another tree. In the process, he kicked Brad and Audrey's four-legged friend, which promptly raised its tail and squirted a stream of foul-smelling liquid onto Cornelius Calhoun.

"A skunk!" he raged, running from the black and white critter, momentarily forgetting about the rifle shots.

"Now," whispered Brad, and Audrey shot again,

shattering a stick holding two ropes together, which, of course, released a sapling loaded with thorny blackberry vines.

"Ahhhh," Calhoun screamed in pain, stumbling and thrashing against the thorny vines clinging to his clothes and tearing his face and hands.

Brad and Audrey carefully aimed and started shooting again, causing Calhoun to thrash even more against the embrace of the thorny vines and, of course, seek shelter. In his effort to escape the bullets whizzing around him, he didn't look where he was going and was caught on one of Brad's many trip ropes, sending him headlong into a clump of blackberry vines.

Screaming in pain and cursing in anger, Calhoun dropped his pistol as he tried to escape the thorny embrace of the vines, all the while gagging on the unique aroma of the skunk's gift to the unwary.

"Cover me," said Brad. "And don't take any chances. I don't want to get hurt."

"Don't worry. Having learned what he had planned for me, I won't hesitate."

Brad rushed to the campsite where he cautiously approached the cursing, screaming, stinking man wrapped in blackberry vines. Hiding Calhoun's pistol behind a rock, Brad approached slowly.

Picking up a large stick, he jammed it into Calhoun's back and said in a firm whisper, "Put your hands behind your back, keep your head down, and don't move."

Calhoun complied as Brad quickly tied his feet together, and then his hands. Retrieving the pistol, Brad started removing the vines from Calhoun. When the last of the vines had been removed, Brad ordered, "Now, roll over, and scoot up to that tree."

Calhoun turned over, blinked in disbelief at seeing Brad, then shouted, "What? You're that Benton kid."

"That's right," said Brad coldly, motioning with the pistol. "Now scoot over to that tree."

"I don't have to do anything for you," spat Calhoun.

"That's your choice." He stepped back and shouted, "Target practice time!"

From her hidden position, Audrey placed her first shot about a foot from Calhoun's bound feet. Calhoun pulled back, a shocked look on his face. Moments later, Audrey's second shot was about six inches from his feet.

"Shall I make it stop?" asked Brad.

"You wouldn't shoot a tied and unarmed man," protested Calhoun half-heartedly.

"You're right. I wouldn't, but my partner would."

Calhoun cocked his head, "What?"

"A little closer this time!" shouted Brad.

Audrey's third shot was about an inch from his foot. Her fourth shot clipped his boot heel.

Brad stooped and examined the boot heel, then shouted, "That's better than last year when you shot the man's foot!"

"I'll move," wailed Calhoun, starting to scoot along the ground to the tree that Brad had pointed toward.

Brad took his last length of rope and tied Calhoun to the tree, then shouted, "He's tied up. Come on down, partner."

Audrey came down and handed one of the two rifles

143

she was carrying to Brad. "You stink," she said, looking Cornelius Calhoun directly in the eye.

"I'm an upstanding citizen," he said trying to sound confident. "You had better release me immediately, or I'll press charges and have you, your brother, and your parents thrown in jail!"

"I will not release you," said Brad. "But, if you're fortunate, I may tell the sheriff where to find you. You kidnapped my sister. You told your partner, Jake Rawlins, to abandon her in the mountains after she saved the lives of your wounded men. You came here to kill us. You told your men to kidnap me like they did my sister. You're lower than the skunk that sprayed you."

"I don't know what you're talking about," blustered Calhoun trying to sound sure of himself. "Release me now!"

While Calhoun continued pleading and threatening, Brad saddled their horses, led them to Calhoun's tree, and looped their reins over a branch. Then he retrieved Calhoun's horse, and tied its reins to a lead. Unlooping the reins of Audrey's horse from a branch, he handed them to her. After she had mounted up, he handed her the lead to Calhoun's horse.

"I'll leave you like this for the wolves and bears," vowed Audrey in a clipped and steely voice. "I'll treat you just like Jake Rawlins' old partner, Duke Badger, did my Pa. Maybe the wolves or the bears will listen to your pleas. I won't."

"Then you're the kids that tracked Duke Badger and rescued their father?"

"That's right."

"And now I've tracked you down and rescued my sister," said Brad. "Goodbye."

Brad mounted his horse and the two Bentons rode away from the miserable human being, tied to a tree, cursing about his fate, unable to escape from the scent provided by the waddling black and white kitty.

CHAPTER 17

Saturday, late afternoon, 11 June 1881: Brad and Audrey had just about reached the junction of the abandoned mine road and the road to Denver when they heard a horse galloping toward them.

"I'm not sure but it looks like Sheriff Strong," said Audrey.

"I think you're right," said Brad.

"Brad! Audrey!" shouted the sheriff, reining his tired horse to a stop. "Thank the Lord you're all right. I received word about an hour ago that Cornelius Calhoun suspected something had gone wrong and that he was probably looking for you."

"We know," said Brad. "He's at the campsite tied to a tree. This is his horse"

"Calhoun's at the campsite?" The sheriff looked at the riderless horse, not quite believing what Brad had said.

"That's right," said Audrey. "And he's a mighty miserable man. He stinks."

"We know that," said the sheriff. "The Pinkertons learned quite a bit about that skunk this morning."

"You're right about his being a skunk," laughed Brad. "Audrey is right, he's miserable and he really stinks."

146

"Most outlaws are miserable human beings," said the sheriff.

"Let me tell you about Mr. Calhoun," said Audrey.

After she finished telling about the blackberry vines, the skunk, and being left tied to a tree, the sheriff was laughing so hard tears were coming down his face.

Earl rode up to the trio to see the sheriff laughing and Brad and Audrey with big smiles on their faces. "All right," he said. "What's so funny?"

"They captured Cornelius Calhoun," said the sheriff, gasping for breath.

"That's great," said Earl, "But, what's funny about that?"

Brad and Audrey retold how Calhoun was captured and Earl began laughing too.

Karl rode up and found the sheriff and Earl, laughing. "I seem to have missed the telling of a marvelous story," he said.

"You certainly did," confirmed the other Pinkerton.

Brad and Audrey told the story of Calhoun's capture for the third time. And, as one would expect, the retelling was interrupted several times by laughter from Earl and the sheriff. When the laughter finally subsided, they realized they had a problem.

"We'll have to burn his clothes and wash him in the creek," said Karl.

"We don't want to take him into town stark naked," said Earl. "But we don't have any extra clothes with us."

"I have a suggestion," said Brad. "It's pretty cruel but I don't know what else we can do."

"And what's that?" asked the sheriff.

"We have the blankets from our bedrolls. But the harsh wool against bare skin for an hour's ride would really be nasty. And if he rides with his bare skin against the saddle, he'll get terrible blisters."

"He can wear what's left of my petticoat," offered Audrey. "It's already ruined. We can just cut it down the side so it will fit around his waist. That would protect him from the harsh wool of the blankets and blistering from the saddle."

"I think that is an excellent idea," said the sheriff. "Karl, Earl, take care of the prisoner. I'll wait here with Brad and Audrey."

"With pleasure," laughed Karl. "This is an assignment we look forward to."

Brad, Audrey, and the sheriff listened to shouts of anger and curses as Calhoun was disrobed, and his clothes burned.

"A petticoat!" screamed Calhoun.

"That's right," ordered Karl. "Either that, or we'll tie you over the saddle, belly down. If you choose to sit in the saddle, we'll wrap the blankets around you. The choice is yours."

U

A little later, the trio emerged from the campsite. Calhoun was tied to his horse, the blankets wrapped around him and held in place with ropes. He sat in his petticoat, the white muslin protecting his legs from chafing on the saddle.

"We've got a long ride ahead of us," said Sheriff Strong. "I'm already getting hungry so let's head out."

Brad, Audrey, and Sheriff Strong led the way, three

abreast, followed by Calhoun with a Pinkerton on each side. The ride back to Denver was uneventful. The interesting part was dismounting at the sheriff's office.

"He's wearing a petticoat!" shouted a man as the Pinkertons helped Calhoun off his horse.

"Did you catch the Petticoat Bandit, Sheriff?" asked another man.

To make matters worse David Girard, the newspaper publisher, arrived as Calhoun was being led into the jail. "The Petticoat Bandit!" declared Girard. "That has a nice sound to it. Can you tell me about it, Sheriff?"

"Don't ask me," said the sheriff. "Ask the two Pinkertons and their young assistants."

"Brad! Audrey!" he exclaimed. "You helped capture the Petticoat Bandit?"

"Excuse me," corrected Detective Braunsohn. "They didn't help capture him; they did capture him. All we did was bring him in."

"Would you be interested in writing your own story about his capture?" asked the newspaperman.

"Brad?" Audrey looked at her brother.

"Yes, we would. We'll leave the margins wide and skip lines for your editing. How is Sunday evening? Then you can include it in your Monday morning edition."

"Excellent," said the newspaperman. "I'll see you Sunday evening."

"Sheriff," said Karl, "Earl and I will take care of things here if you want to pick up your prisoners from the fort."

"Brad, Audrey," asked the sheriff. "Are you up to going to the fort with me? I'll bring a deputy too, of course."

"Yes," replied Audrey. "I'd like to see that snake, Rawlins, again. I want to be the one that tells him that Brad and I caught Cornelius Calhoun."

Sheriff Strong continued, "If we leave now, we can be back by dinner time. The commander offered me the use of a driver and wagon to bring the Rawlins gang to my jail."

"I'm looking forward to dinner with Ma tonight," said Audrey, mounting her horse.

"Me too," said Brad, unlooping his reins.

"It's settled then," said the sheriff. "Let's go."

As the prisoners left the stockade, they held out their hands. A soldier cuffed each man, then another soldier led each prisoner to the wagon. Sheriff Strong, Brad, and Audrey helped the men into the wagon, where they were chained to each other and then to the wagon.

"Thank you again for your help," said the sheriff. "And remember, the Pinkertons promised the guards two free nights at the hotel, including breakfast and supper. They insisted that I remind you of their promise to your guards."

"I'll tell their sergeant," promised the commander. "This is something he'll want to announce in front of all the men."

"Ho!" called the driver, gently flicking the reins. The pair of horses leaned into their collars, and the Rawlins Gang began their trek to the sheriff's office.

"Ma's going to be mighty happy to see you," said Brad.

"I'm going to really give Ma a piece of my mind," said Audrey.

"What!" exclaimed her brother. "Did you just say you were going to give Ma a piece of your mind? Why?"

"I'm going to tell her she needs to take some more shooting lessons from Pa. After all, if her shot at Rex Reed had been better, I wouldn't have been kidnapped."

"But Audrey, she hit him with a .32 pistol at a distance of about 50 feet. That's very good shooting. She only had a few seconds to open her purse, get the gun, aim, and fire. And remember, Rex was a moving target."

"I know; Rex Reed couldn't believe that she even hit him at that distance. But she's my Ma, and I have to tease her about it - just a little."

"What you're really doing is complimenting her for being such a good shot."

"Exactly. I'm mighty proud of Ma for hitting him at all under the circumstances."

As they entered the city, people watched the soldier driving the wagon of men down the street. Sheriff Strong and Deputy McMurray rode in front of the wagon while Brad and Audrey rode behind.

"I think the excitement is about to begin again," said Brad, reining his horse to the hitching rail in front of the sheriff's office.

"I want to be in the outer office when the Rawlins Gang meet Calhoun and smell him," giggled Audrey.

"One at a time," ordered Deputy McMurray, taking the first prisoner from the back of the wagon.

The Pinkertons helped Sheriff Strong move the prisoners into jail cells one at a time. Brad and Audrey

151

stayed in the outer office as the men were led to the cells in back.

"Ohhh, what's that horrible smell!" demanded Curt Bender as he entered the jail area.

"You'll find out soon enough," said the sheriff.

Similar responses came from each gang member as they were led to the cells.

By the time Jake Rawlins was led in, all the men were complaining about Cornelius Calhoun, cursing him for smelling so bad.

"Well," said the sheriff, "You men have no one to blame but yourselves. When you take a skunk as a partner, you don't have any right to complain about the smell."

CHAPTER 18

Sunday morning, 12 June, 1881: Brad, Audrey, and Nurse McLean selected an empty pew near the front of the church and sat down. Brad and Audrey looked around, finding it so much larger than their church in Riverton. They examined the large stained-glass windows, the impressive cross, the huge altar, and row upon row of pews.

"The prelude is about to begin," whispered Audrey.

"What a large piano," said Brad. "Ma said it's called a grand piano."

The music started. The congregation fell silent and listened to their weekly allotment of magnificent music. The piano prelude was played by one of Percival Vaughan-Williams's students. As the congregation rose for the processional, Mr. Vaughan-Williams began playing the opening hymn on the organ. Brad and Audrey listened to the blend of organ and voices as the choir members processed through the church, finally taking their seats next to the grand piano and organ.

After the introit, gospels, and lessons, the Episcopal priest began his sermon. Brad and Audrey didn't pay much attention, but instead continued to absorb the beauty of the stained-glass windows, the tapestry, and the massiveness of the church. Nurse McLean, seated

153

between them, poked them when the sermon was drawing to an end.

"I expect that almost everyone in this congregation heard about the kidnapping of a young lady earlier this week," said Father Thatcher. "But what you don't know is that the mother of that young lady, Abby Benton, will be playing the postlude today. She with other pianists, mostly from churches in Colorado, have been studying with Mr. Vaughan-Williams this week."

The nurse squeezed Brad and Audrey's hands. Brad looked at the choir and saw his mother sitting next to Marion Carter from the library in the alto section. He also saw David and George Girard in the tenor section.

"I expect most of you don't know," continued Father Thatcher, that Mrs. Benton's kidnapped daughter, Audrey, was rescued by her brother and two Pinkerton detectives on Friday. They knew that the men who kidnapped her were the same men that had robbed the bank Tuesday afternoon. So Brad, Audrey and two Pinkerton detectives, who had been deputized by Sheriff Strong, proceeded to capture the Rawlins Gang. After they had captured the gang, Brad and Audrey captured a Denver businessman who had recently become Jake Rawlins' partner in crime. These two outstanding young citizens are with us today. Audrey, Brad, please stand up so we may thank you. Let's give them a big round of applause."

Brad and Audrey, their faces flushed with embarrassment, as well as pride, slowly stood up to a standing ovation and thunderous applause from the congregation and Father Thatcher.

When the service concluded the priest told everyone

to go in peace and Mrs. Benton began the postlude. Men and women Brad and Audrey had never met before, and probably would never meet again, came up and congratulated them.

A tall man in a Stetson hat was one of the last men to see Brad and Audrey. "So you're the little lady that saved the life of Virgil Collins. I'm Brett Grimes, the man that shot Jesse Rebhorn and some of the men you were kidnapped to treat."

"One of the men you shot, Clete Corbin, is in jail," said Audrey. "When I removed your bullet, he apologized for shooting at me. He said he was scared."

"What about the others?" he asked.

"Chite Hobbs died," replied Audrey, a tear running down her face. "I couldn't remove the slug, and the wound festered despite cleaning it with carbolic acid."

"For a man that shot at you, I don't understand why you're so saddened by his death," said Brett.

"He told me to try to escape," confessed Audrey. "He said that Jake Rawlins was going to abandon me in the mountains to die. Two other gang members, Rex Reed and Clete Corbin, were going to help me, if and when there was a chance. But Brad climbed into a second-story window during a gun battle and rescued me."

"That's not all," said Brad, putting his arm around his sister. "Tell him the rest."

"After we had captured the gang members, Chite called to me from the house, told me it was safe to come in. He was lying on a table, very near death. He thanked me again for helping him make his peace with the Lord that morning. I held his hand as he died,"

155

choked Audrey, tears now streaming down her face as they moved down the aisle toward the narthex.

"You gave the man comfort when he needed it," consoled Nurse McLean, putting her arm around Audrey as they approached Father Thatcher. "That is part of ministering to those in need, whether it is ministering as a doctor or as a decent citizen. Death comes to us all. You ministered to a man in need."

"Yes, you did minister to his needs," acknowledged Father Thatcher. "The Lord allows us to make choices, to choose between good and evil. Chite Hobbs chose evil. He was shot and died early in his life. However, before he died you helped him realize that his choice had not been a good one. He asked forgiveness for a bad choice and you helped him find that forgiveness. You treated his body and his soul. That is what you needed to do."

"You did what?" exclaimed Brett Grimes over lunch at Delmonico's Restaurant.

"We did," said Brad.

"You really mean it?" questioned the nurse in disbelief.

"Yes," said Audrey. "Cornelius Calhoun's entire body was scratched from the blackberry vines, he smelled from the skunk spraying him, and all he had on was my ruined petticoat when we took him to jail."

"Maybe his attorney can claim that because his client experienced cruel and unusual punishment, the kidnapping charges should be dropped," laughed the rancher.

"The Rawlins Gang is a rough bunch," Deputy Black chimed in. "When I checked on them this morning, they were all teasing Calhoun mercilessly."

"What were they saying?" asked Abby.

"They're calling him The Petticoat Bandit that got captured by a girl. Some of the men are calling him Skunk Man because he still smells like a skunk."

"His greed caused him to bring it on himself," stated Nurse McLean.

"He's in his own cell now," he continued. "Several of the gang members beat him when they learned he had ordered Audrey to be abandoned in the mountains."

"So there is honor among thieves," said the nurse.

"Even in the Rawlins Gang," conceded Mrs. Benton.

"Wellllll," said Brett some time later. "That was a marvelous Sunday lunch, and the inside story about the capture of the Rawlins Gang made it even better."

"Well that's not quite all," added Audrey.

"You mean you've held something back?" questioned Nurse McLean as she looked at Audrey and then Brad.

"Well, not exactly," explained Brad. "You see, David Girard asked us to write the story for his newspaper."

"We're supposed to deliver it to him tonight so he can include it in tomorrow's paper," said Audrey.

"You're going to include the part about the skunk and the petticoat?" Nurse McLean's eyes brightened with a mischievous smile.

"Definitely," said Audrey. "I will show no mercy to that skunk."

"Now that I've heard the whole story, I can go back to my ranch," said Brett Grimes. "If anything else develops, please tell me at Thursday night's concert."

"Nothing else had better happen," insisted Audrey. "I want to get a new dress, a new petticoat, and, well, be a lady of leisure during the rest of our vacation in Denver."

"Is that what you want to do too, Brad?" asked the rancher.

"Yes, and maybe go back to Wong's Cafe for a Sheriff Strong special."

"Enjoy the rest of your vacation," said the rancher as Nurse McLean took his arm and they prepared to leave. "We'll see you again on Thursday."

"And there will be no man with a big round head to worry about," added Brad.

CHAPTER 19

Thursday Evening, 16 June, 1881: "So that's what a pipe organ sounds like," said Audrey. "I couldn't hear it that well with everyone singing last Sunday. Nana told me what they sounded like and now I know."

"It's like a herd of violins, trumpets, tubas, and pianos corralled into one big musical cattle drive," described Brad.

"That, uh, is very descriptive," acknowledged Nurse McLean.

"Ma said she would be turning pages for the organist, and she has certainly turned a lot of pages," said Audrey.

"Well, according to the program, Ma's supposed to play next," said Brad.

"Here she comes now," said Audrey, as the audience began their applause. "Ma practiced this so much she had it memorized before we left Riverton."

Brad turned to the nurse and added, "Ma said it sounds much better now."

Mrs. Benton came out, stood beside the piano bench, turned to face the audience, and gave a brief bow of thanks for the applause. Then she sat on the large bench, hung her hands down at her sides for a moment to drain the tension, raised them, and began playing Mozart's "Twelve Variations on 'Ah, vous dirai-je, Maman.'" Mrs. Benton enchanted the audience in Denver just as Mozart had done when he first played it a century before in Europe. It repeats a simple melody, recognizable as *Twinkle, Twinkle Little Star*, twelve times, each repetition different from the last. When music is played well, it is appreciated by all.

The last variation, a fast virtuoso creation, was crisp and clear with a continuous stream of sixteenth notes in the left hand until the last eight measures. Then the left hand broadened to give support to the right hand, which culminated in a two-octave ascent to a final C major chord. The last chord, a quarter note, four notes in each hand, resonated in the sanctuary as her hands hovered in the air a foot above the keys. The moment of silence at the end of her performance also remained suspended in the air like her hands as the audience slowly realized that the performance was over.

Then the audience stood as one, applauding as they rose. Brad and Audrey were as captivated by their mother's performance as the people around them and instinctively stood and applauded this performance worthy of the Lord's house. Their mother stood up, moved out from the piano, bowed, and left the sanctuary. The audience remained standing and continued applauding so she returned for a second bow. When she left the second time the applause gradually subsided and the audience sat down.

The final piece was played by Percival Vaughan-Williams on the organ. After the concert the well-wishers congratulated Abby and the other performers on a memorable evening. Mrs. Benton, visibly tired, met her children, Nurse Christine, Brett Grimes, and Deputy Black in the narthex of the church.

"Abby, you look exhausted!" exclaimed Nurse McLean. "Are you still up for dessert?"

"Up for it? I'm ravenously hungry. I'm ready for a full meal. I was so nervous I ate very little all day. I'm ready to fight Brad for the horses' hooves."

"Then it's a good thing I have a large buggy outside waiting to take us to the hotel cafe," announced Deputy Black.

As soon as they reached the hotel cafe, the host showed them to their table. "Ah," said the waiter, "My friends from Riverton have returned. Do you wish dinner, or just dessert?"

"Dinner for me," said Abby. "What do you have that is ready right now? I'm starving."

"Prime rib," said the waiter. "I can have it in front of you in about five minutes. Does anyone else want dinner?"

"May I have the prime rib, too?" asked Brad, looking at his mother.

"Certainly."

The rest of the group said they'd have coffee, except for Brad and Audrey, who asked for tea with their mother. Dessert would wait until Brad and his mother had finished their dinner.

"Ma, you sounded great tonight, said Audrey. Did Mr. Vaughan-Williams help you that much?"

"Yes, he did. He showed me how to shape the music, to bring it alive. That's why I'm so hungry. Playing a concert is hard work. He taught me to throw the full

161

weight of my body down into the keys when I play a loud chord and how to avoid getting tense."

"Like I do when I chop wood?" related Brad.

"Well," laughed his mother. "That is a good comparison; I'd say a very good comparison."

The waiter arrived with a large serving platter and said, "Your prime rib dinners, three coffees, and three teas. Is there anything else?"

"Dessert when we finish," answered Abby.

"What are you planning to do with the reward money?" asked Nurse McLean when the waiter left.

"I want to go to medical school," said Audrey. "Sheriff Strong said he'd deposit the money in a couple of banks in Denver for us. We've already opened the accounts. He urged us to deposit it in two banks. Then, if one bank fails, we'll still have half of the reward money."

"Medical school," pondered Brett Grimes. "Will they allow a woman to enroll?"

"Well, a few women have already become doctors, and I really want to be a doctor."

"When you get ready, I'll help you," said Nurse McLean. "And I know the doctors at the hospital will help, too. They were really impressed with your treatment of the Rawlins Gang."

"I even heard the doctors talking about Audrey's medical skills while I was recovering," said Dan.

"What are you planning to do with your share of the reward, Brad?" asked Dan.

"I'm not sure yet," said Brad, after finishing his last bite of prime rib. "I've thought about studying engineering so I can build bridges, buildings, maybe do something with that new discovery they call electricity.

162

I hear that it can make light so bright that the night looks like daylight. I also hear that there's a device called an electric motor. It's powered by electricity and can be used to run machinery in manufacturing plants."

"I've heard about that too," said Brett. "They compare the power of the electric motor to the work that a horse can do. They call it horsepower."

"We have to finish school first," explained Audrey. "We have a high school teacher coming to Riverton this summer, the sister of Father O'Brien, Riverton's Catholic priest."

"Pa says the next four years of school will be tough," added Brad. "We'll have to write papers, learn algebra, trigonometry, physics, chemistry, and Latin, and I forget all the other subjects."

The waiter arrived and announced, "I brought a platter of desserts. Please take what you want, courtesy of the hotel. The manager says it is the least he can do to thank you for your capture of the Rawlins Gang. And he also asks that you give his regards to David Acker of the Riverton Hotel."

"We will," said Brad, looking at the German chocolate cake and the cherry pie.

Everyone took a piece of pie, cake, or pudding. Brad was still trying to make up his mind when the waiter said, "You'll like the German chocolate cake," as he put the small plate in front of Brad. "I also think you should try the cherry pie," and put another small plate in front of Brad. "But the chef said he would like you to try his newest creation, banana crème pie," and a third dessert plate was placed in front of Brad. "I'll be back for your comments, Mr. Benton."

Brad looked at the three desserts, then at his mother, whose hand covered her mouth. He looked at Nurse McLean who was shaking her head back and forth in disbelief at the array in front of Brad. Deputy Black and Mr. Grimes were laughing.

"Brad," challenged his sister, "Go ahead; try to eat all three desserts. "But first, may I have some of your banana crème pie?"

Brad pushed the plate towards her. "I'll give you the first bite."

Audrey cut a bite with her fork and put it into her mouth. She savored the bite, then reached for another bite. "It is very good, Brad, thank you."

Everyone at the table had finished their dessert and watched Brad as he ate the last bite of the German chocolate cake. "That German chocolate cake and the banana crème pie are great."

"Well, Mr. Benton," said the waiter appearing beside Brad. "What may I tell the chef about the banana crème pie?"

"Please tell him it was marvelous. It ranks right beside the German chocolate cake."

"Yes, it does," said Audrey. "The banana crème pie is simply delicious. I tried it and it was a new and well, utterly delectable flavor."

"Thank you," replied the waiter, smiling. "I'll tell the chef as soon as I return to the kitchen."

"Maybe he'll write on the menu, 'This pie tasted and declared the best by the young Pinkertons who captured the Petticoat Bandit'," laughed the Deputy.

164

"That was a riveting story in the paper," said Mr. Grimes. "The editor printed your names as authors of the story. How you're famous as newspaper reporters as well."

"Tomorrow we leave on the first stage," said Mrs. Benton. "It's late and I need my Pinkertons rested so they can protect me from marauding outlaws on our trip back to Riverton."

"Ma," implored Audrey as they stood up. "We didn't try to find the outlaws, they found us."

"That's right," agreed Bread, pushing in his chair, "I had to rescue my sister."

"And Brad and the Pinkertons had already captured two of the gang members by the time Brad helped me escape."

"We already had their horses," continued Brad. "Besides, they thought we were Indians. They were afraid of getting scalped."

"We were careful, too," explained Audrey. "We did only what the Pinkertons told us to do."

"I suppose making Jake Rawlins drop his trousers around his ankles was a very good method of keeping him from doing more mischief," granted their mother.

"Thanks, Ma," sighed Audrey. "I knew you'd understand."

"But did you really have to make Cornelius Calhoun crawl around inside a bunch of blackberry bushes and have a skunk spray him?" she asked. "I'm told his face still has scabs on it from the thorns and Rawlins Gang is still complaining about his smell."

"We couldn't just shoot him, Ma," protested Audrey

as they came to the hotel lobby. "Reverend Wesley told us it was wrong to kill someone except in self-defense."

"We knew he was coming," added Brad. "Besides, Pa always said we should use our brains to avoid a fight. We did what Pa told us to do."

"He'll go to prison and be known the rest of his life as the Petticoat Bandit," said Deputy Black.

"He made the choice of evil," said Nurse McLean. "He now has his just desserts and I don't mean banana crème pie or German chocolate cake."

"Especially not banana crème pie," sighed Brad. Mrs. Benton looked around at their new friends. "Thank you again for all your help," said Abby.

"Our pleasure," said Nurse McLean. "Goodnight."

The Bentons went to their hotel room and Brad lit the lamp while his mother closed the door. As soon as Abby went around to the other side of the room, Audrey grabbed her brother's arm and whispered, "Brad Benton! I can't believe that you were able to eat all three of those desserts after a prime rib dinner."

"I didn't think I could, either. I don't even want to think about breakfast. And when we get home, you can have the biggest piece of pie. Goodnight, Audrey."

"Goodnight, Brad."

A NOTE ABOUT - ANNIE OAKLEY

Phoebe Ann Moses, known as Annie Oakley, was born in 1860 in Darke County, Ohio. She was the sixth of eight children: seven girls and one boy. When Annie was six her father was caught in a blizzard, developed pneumonia, and died. Her father's death was the first of many challenges Annie faced and overcame.

By the age of seven, Annie could trap small game just like her father taught her. She dug small trenches, covered them with heavy cornstalks, and filled them with corn to attract pheasants, quails, and squirrels that lived in the woods.

By the age of eight, Annie became a markswoman, killing game with her first shot, hunting with her brother and their father's musket. She used this skill to help feed her family.

Her mother remarried but when Annie was ten her stepfather was killed. Annie's mother couldn't support all her children so she sent Annie to live with the Edingtons who ran the Greenville Infirmary. The Infirmary, commonly called the poorhouse, was for people too old, ill, or poor, to take care of themselves.

A local farmer stopped at the Greenville Infirmary

looking for a girl to help his wife care for their baby boy. Annie accepted the position because she was told that the farmer would send her to school to learn reading and writing.

The farmer, however, had lied. Annie was not permitted to go to school. Instead, she had to work fourteen-hour days, seven days a week. She was beaten and even thrown out of the house during a snowstorm. After a year of trying to please her employer, she ran away and returned to the Edingtons at the Greenville Infirmary. She showed them her scars and told them what had happened. Later she learned that the "Wolf Farmer," as Annie called him, had destroyed letters from Annie's mother and replied to them with descriptions of Annie having an enjoyable time at the farm.

After two years, Annie rejoined her family. Her twice-widowed mother had remarried for the third time and Annie resumed hunting to help feed the family. What the family couldn't eat she sold to a grocer in Greenville to help pay off the mortgage on her family's house.

She sold beaver, raccoon, muskrat, and mink furs to Greenville's fur trader, Frenchy La Motte. Annie brought the Greenville grocer more game than he could sell, so he helped Annie sell it to hotels in Cincinnati. Annie's game was prized by the hotels because she used a rifle, killing birds with a single shot to the head, leaving no buckshot. Each mail day, Annie would send boxes of quail to the Cincinnati Hotel.

In the fall of 1875, Annie, then fifteen years old, visited her sister, Lyda Stein, in Cincinnati. Her sister showed Annie the Cincinnati suburb of Oakley where she was thinking about living. This would later become her stage name.

While visiting her sister, Annie went to a hotel that had bought some of her wild game. Having heard about Annie's shooting skill, the hotel owner invited her to a shooting match with Frank Butler, an expert marksman. Annie accepted the challenge. The winner of the match was to receive a prize of $50.00, a significant sum of money in 1875.

Annie was a petite woman, just five feet tall. At first, Frank Butler thought the match was a joke. His attitude changed after Annie's first shot. Twenty-five clay pigeons were released one at a time, for each shooter, alternating between Frank and Annie. Both of them maintained a perfect score through the first twenty-four pigeons. Then Frank Butler missed and Annie didn't. Annie won the $50.00, a position in Frank Butler's shooting show, and his heart. They got married the next year, 1876.

Frank Butler continued his exhibition shooting and while Annie Moses Butler was not yet as famous as her husband, her shooting skills were well known.

In May 1882, Annie joined her husband on stage as a last-minute substitute for his partner who had become ill. Annie was an instant success. Frank knew she was the star, stating later that she outclassed him.

In 1885 they joined Buffalo Bill's Wild West Show, where Annie met Chief Sitting Bull. The Chief offered to adopt Annie because she looked so much like his daughter who had died. Sitting Bull gave Annie the Indian name 'Watanya Cecila', meaning *Little Sure*

Shot. Annie traveled with Buffalo Bill's show on and off for seventeen years.

In the spring of 1887, the show toured England for the celebration of Queen Victoria's 50th year on the throne. When introduced to the Prince and Princess of Wales, Annie shook hands with the Princess first, even though putting the Prince first was the British custom. She told a reporter that in America it was ladies first. The Prince of Wales was not offended; instead, he was very much impressed with Annie.

In 1887, *The Rifle Queen*, a novel, was published in London. The novel fictionalized Annie shooting bears and wolves and stopping robberies. Despite, or perhaps because of the fiction, the novel helped propel Annie to international stardom.

Thomas Edison, inventor of the motion picture camera, filmed her in the fall of 1894 firing her rifle twenty-five times in twenty-seven seconds and shooting glass balls tossed in the air.

Injuries Annie suffered in a 1901 train wreck in North Carolina caused her to leave the Wild West Show. The wreck proved to be a traumatic experience for her; her hair turned white a few months later.

During World War I, Annie gave shooting exhibitions at Army posts and trained her dog to retrieve money that people had wrapped in their handkerchiefs for the Red Cross.

Throughout her life, Annie contributed time and money to orphanages and other charities. It was her way of helping other children avoid the horrors she had experienced at the hands of the Wolf Farmer.

She died on 3 November 1926, at the age of 66. Her

husband Frank died eighteen days later at the age of 76. Both were cremated and their ashes buried at Brock Cemetery in western Ohio.

In 1935, Barbara Stanwyck starred as Annie in the movie *Annie Oakley.* In 1946 the musical, *Annie Get Your Gun,* started a three-year run on Broadway. It became a movie in 1950. In 1954, Gail Davis starred as Annie Oakley in a fictionalized television series, *Annie Oakley,* that ran until 1957.

From trapping small game at age seven, shooting her first game at age eight, to shooting exhibitions on Army Posts in World War I, Annie proved herself an exceptional woman. She overcame poverty, living in an orphanage, and cruel foster parents. To borrow a U.S. Army recruiting slogan, she became "All she could be," an international star and an American legend. More importantly, she remained a kind, loving woman who helped others by giving her time and money to charities and giving shooting exhibitions for soldiers. Annie Oakley remains an American icon.

A NOTE ABOUT: SISTERS OF CHARITY OF LEAVENWORTH AND DENVER'S ST. JOSEPH HOSPITAL

The Sisters of Charity of Leavenworth was founded in November, 1858, when four Roman Catholic nuns and Mother Xavier Ross arrived in Leavenworth, Kansas. Within a few weeks they were teaching in a boys' school, had opened an academy for girls, and were caring for sick people.

The Sisters of Charity of Leavenworth is a religious order that does charitable works for the Roman Catholic Church. Although independent within the Catholic Church, they often take on charitable tasks as requested by members of the clergy.

In 1864, the Sisters of Charity of Leavenworth opened the first private hospital in Kansas when Sister Joanna Bruner, the first trained nurse in the state, arrived and instructed her fellow sisters in nursing.

The Sisters of Charity of Leavenworth founded Saint Vincent's Hospital of Denver in 1873. The name was changed to Saint Joseph Hospital in 1876. The hospital was started in a house, but quickly moved into a brick building on Market Street that was close to Denver's less reputable business district. Told that their hospital was in a questionable neighborhood, the Sisters replied, "We'll take the question out of the neighborhood."

The hospital moved to its current location, 1835 Franklin Street, just a few years later. Today, it is the largest private teaching hospital in Colorado. In 1996 a 102,000-square-foot addition, the Russell Pavilion, was opened.

The success and rapid growth of St. Joseph Hospital was due in large part to the openness of the Sisters of Charity. As with many great works of music, art, and medicine, they cross denominational boundaries. The Sisters of Charity emphasize openness to patients and staff, regardless of religious affiliation. The result is a high-quality teaching hospital that serves the people of Denver, the State of Colorado, and the surrounding states.

A NOTE ON: WOLFGANG AMADEUS MOZART TWELVE VARIATIONS ON "AH, VOUS DIRAI-JE, MAMAN"

Born on January 27, 1756 in Salzburg, Austria, the musician known as Mozart was baptized as Joannes Chrysostomus Wolfgangus Theophilus Mozart. His first names, Joannes Chrysostomus, are in memory of the day of his birth, which is the feast day of St. John Chrysostom.

Wolfgang Amadeus Mozart, child prodigy and musical genius, was a small, thin and rather sickly individual, possibly because he was fed barley water, a reportedly highly nutritious beverage, rather than his mother's milk. He also had rheumatic fever, called soldiers fever in the 18th and 19th centuries, several times as a child. His physical frailty and musical skills made his father, Leopold, very protective of his son.

On Wolfgang's first concert tour at age six, his father banked a sum in one week equal to his own yearly salary as Kapellmeister for the Archbishop of Salzburg.

In 1767, the Mozart family made a concert tour to Vienna, Austria. Soon after they arrived, there was a smallpox epidemic that killed the Archduchess, for whom the young Mozart was to play. Wolfgang and his sister, Marianne, also came down with smallpox. The pox made him so ill that he was blind for over a week and couldn't use his eyes for several weeks after that.

In September 1768, Wolfgang and his mother departed Salzburg for a tour of Vienna, southern Germany, and Paris, France. While in Vienna, Wolfgang, then age 12, met and fell in love with 16-year old Aloysia Weber, who was related to the well-known composer, Carl Maria von Weber. Wolfgang's father, however, quashed the romance.

In March of 1778, Wolfgang and his mother went to Paris. Some historians believe that Wolfgang wrote two sets of piano variations for his students in Paris: K265, "Twelve Variations on "Ah, vous dirai-je, Maman" and K353, "Variations of "La belle Francoise." Other music historian, however, believes these variations were written later, in the summer of 1780, 1781, or 1782. Wolfgang's mother died while they were in Paris and he returned to Salzburg in September 1778.

Leopold Mozart used his daughter, Marianne, to coerce Wolfgang into supporting his family. Leopold feared that since Wolfgang was an adult, he would marry and start his own family, shifting his allegiance away from his father. Expressed as a parable, Wolfgang Mozart was a goose laying golden eggs, and if he married, Wolfgang's wife would receive the golden eggs. Greed does strange things to people, and in this case, greed caused Leopold Mozart to take devious and un-fatherly actions to keep control of his son.

In 1781, at the age of 25, Wolfgang finally broke

ties with his father and the Archbishop of Salzburg and settled in Vienna. There he met and fell in love with Constanze Weber, the sister of the woman he met 1777. They were married on August 4, 1782.

In the summer of 1791, a stranger, believed to have been Count Walsegg, commissioned Mozart to write a Requiem Mass (a mass for the dead). It is believed that Count Walsegg intended to pass off the work as his own composition. The Count had commissioned musical works from other composers and then had them published under his own name.

Unfortunately, Mozart, then age 35, became ill and told his wife he feared that he had been poisoned. He became weaker and weaker. By November 15, 1791, he was bedridden and in constant pain, his hands and feet swelling from the fever. Two highly regarded Viennese physicians treated him and stated that the rumors that he had been poisoned by Salieri, a bitter rival, were false.

Mozart died in Vienna on December 5, 1791 of rheumatic fever, a disease he had experienced several times in his childhood. The date of his burial is recorded as 6 or 7 December, depending upon the source. He was buried in an unmarked grave, a pauper's grave, in St. Marx Cemetery in Vienna, Austria.

BRAD AND AUDREY HELP CAPTURE THE TRAIN ROBBERS!

CHICAGO ROUNDUP

E.D.G. SMITH

FOR AN EXCERPT, TURN THE PAGE.

CHAPTER 1

Monday, 11 July 1881: "The train is slowing, but I don't see a hill or a town," said Audrey.

"You're not the engineer. I'm sure they know what they're doing," said Brad.

"It's just that I don't understand why they're slowing down."

"Maybe they're stopping for water," said Nana. "These steam engines need a lot of water."

"Or maybe some cattle are on the track," added Audrey.

"Or maybe it's a holdup," said Brad. "Two masked men just entered the car."

"Just keep your seats, and no one will get hurt," said a masked man in a raspy voice as he quickly strode down the car. He stopped at the far end and turned around. He looked at Audrey. "You, the young lady with the blond hair. Take this bag."

The man tossed a large canvas bag toward Audrey. Instinctively, Audrey caught the bag, never looking away from the criminal.

"As the girl passes among you, place your watches, rings, money, other valuables, and guns, if you have them, in the bag. Don't try keep anything because I'll

179

be checking each of you. And don't try any gunplay unless you want to see how well I can shoot this pistol."

The man looked at Audrey through the holes that had been cut in his bandana and motioned with his pistol for her to stand and start down the aisle.

Audrey slowly stood up, opened the bag, and approached the first passenger, an elderly man with a cane. The man slowly extracted his wallet, removed all his bills, and dropped them into the bag. Then, he reached into his inside jacket pocket and moved a small leather purse and dropped it into the bag.

"Good job, old man," said the raspy-voiced man. "You're next," he said pointing his pistol at a well-dressed lady in the next seat. "The rest of you can speed things up by getting all your valuables out now."

In a few minutes, all the passengers had put their valuables in the canvas bag. Audrey handed the bag to the man and returned to her seat.

"Thank you for letting me keep the locket my husband gave me," said a middle-aged woman, tears streaming down her eyes. "It's all I have left to remember him by."

The robber nodded in response, looked at the widow, and said in a soft and gentle voice, "The war was a cruel experience for everyone, ma'am, North and South." He raised his head and looked at the passengers, then announced in a loud voice, "Everyone lay on the floor, face down. Don't look up, or get up, until the train starts moving. If you do, my partners and I may have to start shooting. And if we start shooting, someone may get hurt. Get down! Now!"

Everyone quickly obeyed and laid down on the floor. The passengers heard footsteps, the nickers of horses, and the creaking of saddle leather as the robbers mounted their horses.

"Stay down," said Brad, looking around the car. "The leader was nervous, who knows..." Brad's sentence was cut short by two gunshots, one of the shots splintering the wood of the car roof.

"I presume," whispered Audrey "that you feared they might start shooting even if we stayed down."

"You presumed correctly, and I was right." Brad's reply was quickly followed by the sound of horses spurred to a gallop, the hoof beats fading away.

"Is anyone hurt?" asked Nana, slowly getting up from the floor.

There was flurry of conversation as people checked on those near them. "It appears that everyone in this car is all right," said a well-dressed woman. "We should check the next car; someone may need help."

The door connecting the passenger cars opened and a young man shouted, "A man is hurt! Is there a doctor here?"

Everyone looked around at each other. Then Audrey replied, "If there's not a doctor, I'll help. I've done quite a bit a doctoring lately."

Brad and Audrey went to the adjacent car to find a man laying on the floor, his shirt had a slowly widening patch of red.

"I need some pillows, blankets, or folded coats - now!" shouted Audrey as she knelt beside him.

Several folded blankets quickly appeared and Audrey placed one under the man's head. Brad pulled out his pocket knife, opened it, and handed it to his sister. "I didn't give it to the robber."

"Does anyone have some whiskey?" said Audrey, looking up at the men around her.

"I have a flask of bourbon," said a man with a heavy southern accent, opening a valise and removing a glass bottle. Audrey took the bottle and removed the cork.

"Harry Beam is my name. I'm a liquor salesman. One of my clients makes the finest Kentucky bourbon. I've got more if you need it."

Looking into the wounded man's eyes, she said, "I'm going to pour some of this onto your wound. It will help reduce the spread of infection until we get you to a doctor. Now this is really going to hurt. Are you ready?"

"One is never ready for pain, young lady. Do what you have to do. I'll refrain from screaming," said the man, his face paled from the wound.

"Brad," said Audrey, "put something like coats or blankets under his legs, I need to raise them above his heart."

Using her brother's knife, she cut the shirt away to expose the wound. Then she poured some of the bourbon on the wound. The man gasped but did not scream at the sudden pain.

"I think I can remove the slug," said Audrey. "Would you like me to try, or would you rather wait until we reach Chicago?"

"You're better than the doctors I had in the war, little lady. Do your best and thank you for trying."

"I need another knife, some tweezers, sewing scissors, small tools - anything like that will help," said Audrey.

A woman quickly handed her a small pair of sewing scissors. Another salesman opened his sample case and said," I'm a hand-tool salesman, Miss. Perhaps you can use these, a pair of needle nose pliers used by jewelers."

"I'm making some bandages now," said the lady with the sewing kit. "I need a knife to start a tear in the cloth; is there another knife here?"

A rancher pulled out a large knife and handed it to the lady. "They didn't search me, and I didn't offer it," he said, looking at the other passengers. "Besides, they already got my pocket money and pistol, the thieving snakes."

"I don't believe in drinking," said Audrey to the wounded man, "but you may want to drink some of this bourbon before I start probing for the bullet."

"I'll take the pain of your probing rather than experience again the pain of the spirits. Do your best, little lady."

Audrey wiped the scissors, Brad's knife, and the pliers with a bourbon-soaked cloth. Then, she began her search for the bullet. "I found it," Audrey said softly as she held the point of the scissors in the wound with her left hand. With her right hand, she picked up the jeweler's pliers and reached into the wound. She slowly pulled out the slug as they heard two long blasts of the train's whistle.

"Now for the piece of your shirt," she said. The train jerked and slowly started moving. Bracing her hands on the man's chest, Audrey daubed away the blood that was oozing out of the wound and probed gently with her little finger until she found the scrap of cloth. The train rocked back and forth as it gained speed. She once again took the jeweler pliers, ran them down the front of her finger to her fingernail, gripped the scrap of cloth, closed the pliers, and gently pulled out the piece of the man's shirt.

"Now you'll need these," said the woman who had been preparing the bandages. "I have two more ready, if you need them. And here are some longer strips to hold it in place. I made them from an old petticoat."

Audrey wiped the wound clean with another bourbon-soaked cloth, then applied the bandage. "Brad, pass the cloth strips underneath him and I'll tie them over the wound."

Brad passed three long strips under the man, who grimaced but continued to remain silent. The woman handed Audrey another bandage, larger than the first one. She accepted it, securing it over the wound by knotting the strips into place.

"You're just like my Pa," said Audrey. "He didn't say anything when I bandaged his wound, though I didn't remove the slug from his wound. Now that you're bandaged, let me introduce myself. I'm Audrey Benton, and this is my brother Brad."

"Preston Wood, but just call me Woody, everybody else does."

"Well, Woody, I recommend that you continue laying on the floor until we get to Chicago. Then we can get you to a doctor."

The conductor who had been watching Audrey said, "At the next stop I'll wire Chicago for an ambulance."

"Thank you," said Audrey.

Woody looked at Audrey, "Well, Doctor, may I have some water? I'm rather thirsty."

A passenger handed Woody a canteen of water. "You

bring your own food and water or do without. Besides, the food available at the stops is often questionable."

"That was some good doctoring," said a woman standing behind Audrey. "My husband is a doctor, and I've watched him work on wounded men. I would like to talk to you. I'll be in the other car when you finish."

"I dampened a spare bandage so you can clean your hands," said the first woman, handing it to Audrey.

Audrey stood up, holding onto the back of a seat. "Brace him with luggage, coats, and blankets to keep him comfortable. He mustn't use his muscles to keep from rolling side-to-side with the movement of the train. I'll be in the next car if you need me," said Audrey, wiping the blood from her hands.

Brad and Audrey returned to their seats in the other passenger car to find Nana with the doctor's wife.

"According to your grandmother, you've done quite a bit of doctoring for a lady of your age. I'm Constance Fowler. My husband is the Dean of the Northerwestern University School of Medicine. Tell me about your treatment of the Rawlins Gang last month."

Audrey told her about being kidnapped, treating the wounded men, and the death of Chite Hobbs. Brad told Mrs. Fowler about their father and Jim Bates, the stagecoach driver, who were both shot by Duke Badger. "And I helped deliver Mrs. Wesley's baby this spring," added Audrey.

They talked for sometime while Nana sat in another seat talking with a woman she had met earlier. "We're getting closer to Chicago; we'd best get ourselves organized," said Mrs. Fowler. Please do call on me during your stay. This is my husband's card; I've written our address on the back. I expect to meet you for lunch at Marshall Field's restaurant on Tuesday at noon."

"Yes, ma'am, we look forward to meeting you under more pleasant circumstances," said Brad. Mrs. Fowler returned to her seat.

"Brad, Audrey," said Nana. "I'd like you to meet Mrs. McCormick. We've been making notes about the robbers. I'm sure your Uncle Henry will want the information."

"Oh!" said Audrey. "We were so busy taking care of the wounded man that I forgot all about that."

"Welllll," drawled Brad reaching into his pocket for a small notebook and pencil. "There had to be at least five men, two in each passenger car and one in the engine."

"One of the men in this car had a slight limp," said Audrey taking the notebook and pencil from her brother. "And the man with the canvas bag had a raspy voice."

They discussed the robbery and wrote down the information that Nana and Mrs. McCormick had talked about. Then they went to the other passenger car to gather more information.

"Mr. Wood," said Audrey, kneeling beside her patient. "How are you feeling?"

"Much better that I did the last time I was shot. But I had better doctoring this time."

"When were you shot before?" asked Audrey.

"In the Civil War, or as some folks in the south say, the War of Northern Aggression. A Yankee artillery shell knocked me down, cut my back up pretty bad."

"I'm sorry," said Audrey. "My Pa was in the war, too. He was in the Union Army."

"The war is over. We're one nation, we must never let anything separate us again," replied Woody.

"That's right," said Harry Beam. "I, too, fought for the South. But the war is over, we've made our peace and we must look to the future, not to the past."

"We're making a list of descriptions about the robbers. What can you tell us about them?" asked Audrey.

"There were five of them," said Woody. "I stood up when I heard them mount their horses, that's when one of the men shot me."

Brad looked at the liquor salesman. "Didn't they tell you to stay on the floor until the train started moving?"

"No, they just thanked us for our valuables as they left."

"You were shot with a .38 caliber pistol. You're fortunate," said Audrey. A .45 would have penetrated farther and been much harder to remove. A .45 may have even killed you."

"Come now, little lady. How do you know about gunshot wounds?" asked Woody.

"I've doctored a number of men that have been shot. Most recently, several members of the Rawlins Gang."

"I heard about that, but that was over in Colorado, near Denver," said Harry Beam.

"Were you the young lady they kidnapped?" asked Woody.

"Yes," said Audrey. "And I don't ever want to go through that again."

Brad and Audrey briefly told Woody and the other

passengers about Duke Badger shooting their father, and Audrey's kidnapping by the Rawlins Gang.

"How is your patient?" asked Mrs. McCormick as they returned to their seats. Mrs. Fowler turned in her seat on the other side of the aisle to hear their answer.

"He's fine," said Audrey. "He confirmed Brad's guess that there were five robbers. He stood up and looked at them when he heard them mount their horses. That's when they shot him."

"They didn't tell the folks in his car to stay on the floor. They just thanked them for their valuables," added Brad.

"Your grandmother was telling me why you're traveling to Chicago," said Mrs. McCormick. "It was to be a pleasant experience after the kidnapping in Denver. I'm sorry you got off to a bad start with a train robbery."

"Ma's not going to believe it," said Brad. "She'll think we did something to attract the robbers."

"Not after I tell her what happened," said Nana. "I'll make sure she realizes that you were just passengers on a train that got robbed."

"Thanks, Nana," said Audrey. "Thanks in advance for sticking-up for us."

"We have Father O'Brien's package to deliver to his old bishop," said Brad. "And Nana has some old friends to visit."

"Let me give you my address," said Mrs. McCormick. "Your grandmother and I are planning on having dinner at the Palmer House Thursday, at 6:00 pm. If you're not chasing outlaws, you're invited."

"We are not going to be chasing outlaws, are we, Brad?" said Audrey, defiantly crossing her arms over her chest as she stared at her brother.

Brad looked at his sister's firm face. "We would really like to have dinner with you, Mrs. McCormick. And my sister is correct, we are not going to be chasing outlaws."

ACKNOWLEDGEMENTS

Many thanks to Lora Cooper for her editing, suggestions and helping to bring **Denver Music** to completion. Lora is a museum educator who lives and works in Charlottesville, Virginia. She holds a B.A. in History from Christopher Newport University and a Master of Education from the University of Virginia. Lora has sung with school and church choirs for many years and occasionally records acapella pieces with friends. And to paraphrase a quote attributed to Winston Churchill, Lora identified some grammarizing up with which she would not put. And thanks to Kathryn Boudreau, and her dog Daisy, for taking photos and providing encouragement.

OTHER TITLES BY THIS AUTHOR

The Bigfoot Gang

Captive

Fiery Blizzard

Healer Gang

Denver Music

ABOUT THE AUTHOR

Born and raised in the West, Smith grew up where many farmers still used horses to plow their fields. Steam engines were the norm for railroads, and a diesel locomotive was quite an event. He's now caught up with modern civilization.

After serving in the U. S. Air Force, he later worked as a teacher, professional musician, and federal employee. He has now settled down and lives in Virginia. You can find out more about him at www.edgsmith.com.

CONNECT WITH THE AUTHOR

Website:
www.edgsmith.com

Social Media:
www.facebook.com/edgsmith